Ananya

Ananya

A JOURNEY OF FAITH

Swati Bakshi

PARTRIDGE
A Penguin Random House Company

To order additional copies of this book, contact
Partridge India
000 800 10062 62
www.partridgepublishing.com/india
orders.india@partridgepublishing.com

This book is dedicated to my parents Asit Ranjan Baksi and Lt. Sandhya Baksi.

I miss you maa.

Acknowledgement

Thank you *sanju* and *didibhai* for your tremendous help and support.

Thank you very much *Ben Rosalind* and *Ann Minoza* for your suggestions and guidance.

Last but not the least thank you *Samir*{ [my husband]. Without your encouragement, patience and criticisms this work would not have been possible.

Prologue

December 10, 2013

"Good morning Sam! You have just another half an hour to go . . . .

I'll be waiting in the lawn with the children . . . . so much of work still left and . . . .

Oh God how can you sleep on so comfortably?"

The voice died down the stairs as Samarth groped for the steaming cup of tea on the side table.

Even with half closed eyes he knew exactly where the cup would be with the newspaper and specks right beside it. There was nothing different about it . . . this had been the routine for the last fifteen years ever since Aan had come into his life.

Only one thing she'd manage to change over the years, the two glasses of water in the morning (from the pre-marital years) had given way to morning tea.

Samarth smiled quietly. Actually Aan insisted on enjoying her first cup of tea with her husband and Samarth had most willingly relented.

Aan was worth accepting such changes, he reflected happily.

But this morning was different and Samarth knew it.

The bouquet of fresh white lilies blooming in the crystal vase on the dressing table said it all.

Samarth had come to identify this fragrance over the last fifteen years.

It always came on one particular day . . . . and needless to say it was all Aan's doing . . . . her unique way of reminding him 'aromatically' (as she put it) that it was yet another 8th December.

Sixteen years back they had tied knots on this day, with trepidations, defying law, defying society, defying family.

But that was long long ago and Samarth didn't want to remember it all anymore.

As he pushed aside the blanket that cozily hugged him so long, he also brushed aside those surging memories. He had been just too happy with his Aan and the children and they comprised his world.

'His Aan'. Samarth always loved to think this way . . . . the only one in his life whom he fondly and proudly called 'his'.

A flush of inexplicable joy flooded him over as he gulped down a long sip of tea that was on the verge of cooling now. But he didn't dare ask for a second cup as the clock glared at him severely, its arms showing nine.

Samarth knew he now had exactly fifteen minutes to shave, manage a quick shower, change and get the car out.

Aan would be waiting, dressed in her exquisite red bordered white *Dhakai* sari, wearing no make up except a small red bindi adorning her forehead and a natural shade of lip colour to gloss her lips.

This had been the picture on every 8th December for the last sixteen years and he wouldn't do anything to alter it.

So Samarth hurried. His white *kurta pajama*, wallet, car keys, handkerchief, deodorant . . . everything was on the bed just waiting to be put in the right place.

Aan had indeed spoilt him over the last decade and a half and no denying he loved every bit of that.

Samarth checked the clock. Just three more minutes to go before his committed deadline would be over and he was resolute not to let it happen . . . . at least on this day.

God saved him as *He* had been doing for the last so many years and Samarth breathed a quick prayer of thanks to *Him*.

Finally now he was at the wheels as Aan climbed in beside him making herself comfortable in the classy black leather seats in their Indigo blue Wagon-R with Pihu and Piyal cozying up at the back with sleepy eyes.

9.30 on a December morning was too early for the two otherwise vibrant and vivacious twins.

But they had been groomed to this routine by their mother ever since they started toddling. In fact they didn't seem to mind a deviated routine just once in the whole year. Their mom called it their 'exclusive family day' and they kind of enjoyed it. By now it had become a family ritual for them and none of the quartet in the car wanted to disturb it.

"Happy Anniversary dad", came in the drooling voice of Piyal as Pihu handed to him her self painted card. It was her specialty.

Piyal however always waited for the evening to spring his bit of surprise for his parents.

Samarth knew the kids had already wished their mother at midnight when he was still struggling to wrap up his last bit of work in the office.

By the time he reached home everyday, they were usually in bed. So he always had to wait for his share of wish till the morning.

As Aan held the card open for him, Samarth quickly glanced through it.

The road was too busy to concentrate on the contents at that moment and he hated it. But both father and daughter knew how avidly he would read it once he parked the car outside the premises of their destination.

They were almost there.

Aan beamed to see her *other* children making steadily towards their car.

Like every year they had flowers and *aarti thhalis* and home-made sweets to greet them.

The entire **SAMAN's HOME** seemed to have come alive, decorated with bright, colourful streamers and balloons.

They made it appear like an advanced Christmas celebration every year . . . . and why not? Their Santa Claus had come to them with gifts of love, prayer and blessings.

Samarth and Ananya were the light of their lives . . . . their faith, their hope, their courage.

Pihu and Piyal happily distributed the gifts and the chocolates they had brought loaded in the car.

They always enjoyed coming here.

As the children laughed, played and made merry . . . . Samarth and Ananya simply drank in thirstily with their eyes the pleasure of this scene.

Not a single child seemed an orphan here.

They were all their children . . . . Samarth's and Aan's . . . . **SAMAN'S**.

The celebrations had begun but it was time now to leave.

The preparations for the evening party were still on and things had to be hurried.

JC was to take care of the refreshments and Aan knew she could rely on him blindly.

But she would have to personally supervise the decorations and do it all alone.

Samarth was too pampered by her to do any worthwhile work at home.

Aan was actually happy enough with Samarth managing at least his professional life alone without her help.

Otherwise he was so dependent on his Aan.

She grinned, thinking how she had always considered Sam more as her first child than husband

Chapter 1

THE PARTY
December 10
11:30 A.m.

"Impeccable Aan . . . you just couldn't have been better".
      "I'm not at all impressed Sam . . . . long time . . . .
now at least try and say something different . . . . at least
for a change start helping me out with the arrangements
instead of just smartly shoving in the invitation list in my
hand . . ."

      "Hey not fair Aan. I take care of the toughest job every
year . . . . the guest list you see . . . . got to be careful honey
while making it lest we should leave somebody out . . . .
but you will never appreciate my efforts . . ."

      "What a blatant lie Sam . . . . when have you ever
jotted down a name without bothering me and Pihu
frequently?

      Last year you didn't even spare her during her NTSE
preparations. How soon you forget sweetheart how your
daughter had tried to drill sense into you that her exams
were more important than your guest list . . . ."

      The usual love laden mock fight session was
interrupted by Beena, their middle aged maid announcing
that mom was back.

      Ananya hurried outside, she had to help her
mother-in-law carry the puja thali inside.

1

After all she too hadn't deviated from her routine over the past sixteen years. Every year on this day she has religiously visited the temple and offered puja ceremoniously for her son, daughter-in-law and the grandchildren.

Needless to say the latter were her lifeline.

She was happy; Ananya had proved a good daughter-in-law after all in spite of all her apprehensions.

Samarth was right about her . . . . no girl could have kept her family better woven.

Ananya approached in hasty steps to help her out of the car. She never left these small but delicate responsibilities to servants. She was always a believer in personal touch, whether at work or in relationships.

Not that it had been an easy going in the beginning but eventually things had fallen into place.

Ananya had to admit that with the passage of time she had never let her miss her own mom.

None of the two realized when exactly the 'in-law' term had vanished from between them.

What remained was only a mother called '*ma*' and a daughter called '*anu*', who fought and sort together . . . . laughed and cried together.

Ma was as much Anu's as Samarth's. And they all felt that.

Reaching her to her room, Ananya hurried down. Those in charge of doing up the sprawling lawn with gay looking streamers, colourful kiosks and the necessary sitting arrangements were now almost through with their jobs.

They had been at it since last evening. The electrician guys were still struggling to finish their part within the assigned 2 o clock as per Ananya's strict orders.

Samarth was just too lenient with them, she thought.

In any case she wanted everything ready by 2 ensuring that her family lunched together on their 'exclusive family day' along with her extended family . . . . the decorator, electrician and refreshment boys.

Ananya was the '*didi*' of some, '*bhabi*' of the others and as such they had grown used to her scolding over the years.

None of them could miss that spark of love she nurtured for each of them.

So Chhotu, Bittu, Badal, Raju, Debu, Kishore . . . . all ensured that Ananya had what she wanted.

To her they were the resources she was proud of and to them she was an angel of love.

JC had always been a gem. Without him Ananya felt lost. Originally Samarth's childhood friend, what a brother this man had been to Ananya!

This was the only other relationship besides Samarth's, on the faith of which Ananya had left her home for an unknown world, sixteen years back.

He had been a committed brother ever since. Without him Ananya's family was incomplete.

He was less of her husband's best friend now, and more her brother, always keen to protect her interests.

Satisfied with the proceedings downstairs, Ananya had another major responsibility waiting.

After lunch Samarth had to be literally pushed out of the house . . . . he had to receive Ved, her brother-in-law and Ishita, her sister-in-law.

Ishita's husband was on an official tour so she was coming to attend the function with her four year old son.

Ved, on his way home from the airport, had offered to pick up his sister and nephew.

His flight from Mumbai was to land in the city around 4.30 and Samarth was to drive them home.

Of course Samarth never found any justifiable reason behind this torture. He hated driving and could never understand why his brother and sister couldn't reach home on their own.

But who would explain all that to Aan? It was easier going and finishing the task than reasoning out with Aan. They were her pampered 'bro' & 'sis' in law and she loved spoiling them as much as she spoilt her husband.

Samarth had left. Ma was in her room. JC had gone home for a while to rest and change. Pihu was busy with some friend on the phone. Piyal was busy working on something secretly in his room. In the lawn men were busy doing the final bits here and there.

The afternoon was very quiet. It was a little stuffy. The sky looked slightly gloomy. Not a leaf was moving.

Ananya came and stood in the balcony; alone.

Samarth had designed this balcony especially for her in spite of the crunch of space.

Suddenly she felt a lump in her throat. There was a desperate urge in her to cry. The reason was not unknown to her.

Her parents couldn't come this year. At eighty six, baba couldn't take journeys anymore and ma couldn't possibly leave him alone and come.

It was almost a year now that she had last met them.

Her family and work kept her too tied up to fly down to them as frequently as before.

Did she lose the daughter Annu somewhere in the course of being a dutiful wife, mother and daughter-in-law? The thought blurred her vision suddenly.

"What's up mom?"

She hastily tried to wipe the tears hearing Pihu's voice.

"Nothing", she lied.

"Ok, I had come in to check if you were sleeping . . . . actually dadi was asking for you ".

"Yes I'll just be there". Ananya started towards her mother-in-law's room.

"Mom", Pihu's voice made her stop.

"Mom, why don't you call up *dadai* and amma at kolkata once? I'm missing them".

Ananya walked up to her daughter silently and hugged her tight to her bosom and remained like that, in silence, for quite some time.

Chapter 2

MORAL SCIENCE CLASS
Durgapur, 1970

" . . . . *a*aand it will surprrrise you what the loord haas doneee . . . ."

"Aaaananya" . . . . the rude roar startled the little girl and lashed her back to the cement floor of reality."

"Stand up! Come here . . . . fast".

The little girl stood up, her heart trepidating.

With a parching throat and misty eyes she made it towards her teacher's desk . . . . a large, fat, too white, frozen looking women whose cold eyes sent a chill down her spine.

Her steps faltered and she felt her knees wobbling beneath her.

"Why weren't you paying attention in the class?" she barked.

The little girl tried to murmur something but her voice didn't co-operate. Only some incoherent utterances came out adding to the teacher's fury.

"Stretch out your palm, girl", her voice yelled cruelly again.

The little girl obeyed quietly.

Her face grimaced in pain as the deceptively harmless looking cane came down on her soft palm, turning it red in an instant . . . . and then again it came down . . . . and again . . . . and again . . . . till she started feeling quite numb.

But she didn't cry.

Her eyes refused to shed tears though the lump remained stuck in her throat.

Her little heart revolted as she wanted to cry out "I haven't done anything wrong". But she had lost her voice.

"Now go out to the corridor and kneel down for the rest of the period".

The little girl obeyed again.

As her knees hurt, she whispered to herself, "What is my mistake lord?"

She tried to listen for an answer but there was none.

But how can that be? The little girl wondered.

Sister Mariana had said the other day that if you ask any question to God from your heart, *He* answers. And Sister Mariana couldn't be wrong. She was such an angel herself.

Wasn't she the one who had taught the little Ananya for the first time that God is her best friend? That *He* talks to us anytime we want to? That *He* does miracles to protect those that love *Him*?

"Where are you God?" the little girl's eyes looked around, searching for her best friend faithfully.

But there was no sign of *Him*.

"Have I not called you from my heart?" she wondered again.

"Ananya, my child, what on earth are you doing here? What is wrong?"

The little girl felt her ears grow hot in embarrassment as she heard her angel's voice.

She felt so ashamed to tell Sister Mariana that she had been punished and turned out of the class.

Though just a child of ten, it wasn't difficult for the little girl to understand that the principal of her school was a little partial towards her.

She loved her more than she loved anybody else in the school.

But why they felt so strongly for one another that neither the forty two year old nun nor the child of the fourth standard ever understood.

All that they both realized was that some mysterious bond kept their two souls connected. It was the bond of love and it could not be explained.

"What have you done to be thus punished, child?" Sister Mariana's question confused the little girl."

"I don't know sister. Teacher said I wasn't paying attention."

"And is that true my dear?"

"I don't know sister" . . . . came the honest reply.

"What class were you having Ananya?"

"Moral Science, sister"

"What was your teacher teaching you dear?"

"A poem, sister"

"What poem were you being taught?"

"COUNT YOUR BLESSINGS"

"Can you recite it for me dear?"

"Yes sister"

"Ok Ananya, but first stand up, stretch your legs and then recite the poem for me"

The little girl stood up. Her knees were aching but she didn't want Sister Mariana to understand that.

She wanted to recite for her the poem she had loved so much.

The little girl felt very very happy as she got ready to recite the poem before her angel.

She started . . . .

'When upon life's billows you are tempest tossed
When you are discouraged thinking all is lost
Count your many blessings name them one by one
And it will surprise you what the lord has done
Are you ever burdened with a load of care?
Does the cross seem heavy you are called to bear?
Count your many blessings every doubt will fly
And you will keep singing as the days go by.

Count your blessings name them one by one
Count your blessings see what God has done
Count your blessings name them one by one
And it will surprise you what the lord has done'

"That was very beautiful Ananya. You recited it so beautifully . . . . I'm sure you enjoyed it while it was being taught?

Otherwise you couldn't have recited it so well"

"Yes sister"

"Then what was the problem? What were you doing when the poem was being taught?"

"I was counting my blessings sister."

On her way back to her office, Sister Mariana felt very strange. The ten year old Ananya seemed *Faith* incarnate to her . . . .

On her way back to her class the happy little girl didn't realize that the first miracle had happened in her life.

God had responded to her call. *He* had given her a unique armour of protection called *Faith*.

Chapter 3

Oooooooooof ma! Ananya stretched and turned to her side.

She checked the time in her mobile. It was showing 4.35.

But today Ananya was in no hurry. It was a rare and welcome free evening for her. The institute was closed as the students were having their second terminal examinations and the next day they were to take their History test. So Ananya could jolly well extend her siesta and laze on for some more time.

Sleep was gone so she simply turned on her stomach, pressed her face on the pillow and tried to savour the flavour of this unscheduled free evening.

But in spite of all the challenges and hard work in her profession, Ananya enjoyed it to the core. She missed the children even if classes remained suspended for just a day.

Sushila wouldn't be coming in before 7.30. So Ananya decided to make herself a cup of tea.

It's been quite a long time since she had made anything for herself. Kitchen was one place that somehow appalled her.

Back at home ma always took care of things. Ever since she had shifted out and started living by herself, Sushila had come into her life like an angel.

She was a typical low class *basti* woman who had come to her one day asking for work. She had wept bitterly narrating the common story of how her husband had abandoned her and their four year old son for another woman.

Tears, shed no matter for what reason, never failed to move Ananya. This time however she was touched by the poor woman's resolution to educate her child . . . . to give him a dignified life.

Since then she had stayed with Ananya and the latter had happily borne the educational responsibilities of the child.

Sushila had been no less caring than her mother, always looking into her smallest of needs with the greatest of concern. Needless to say Sushila was never just a maid for Ananya. She was more like an elderly sister and they both had come to love each other over the passage of time.

5.15 . . . the watch said and Ananya craved for the tea.

Though winter had not set in, there was a nip in the air. Ananya wrapped a light cotton shawl around her. It gave her a smug, warm feeling as she proceeded towards her kitchen.

It was a small kitchen space with just a marble slab table top to accommodate her single-burner gas oven, some necessary utensils and containers for provision. In the space below there were the utensils' rack, the water buckets and a small shelf to keep the containers of biscuits, dry snacks, milk powder etc.

Though very small, the kitchen sufficed for her single self. In fact it was quite in keeping with her small single bedroom four hundred square—feet flat.

As the water in the kettle simmered, Ananya put a spoon full of her favourite *Mokaibari-tea* leaves into it, turned the gas off and waited for the familiar flavour to brew. This was her only addiction in life . . . . rich tea . . . aromatic . . . . perfect blend of flavour and liquor. She was extra careful with it always and had it black without sugar.

The only other persons she trusted her tea with, were her mom and Sushila.

Ananya took a short careful sip from the steaming cup. It tasted good. Having had lunch around 12, she felt a little hungry but decided against biscuits or any snacks. That would hamper the flavour of the tea.

There was nothing in particular to do in the evening. For a change there wasn't even any bunch of students' exercise books waiting to be corrected. The tele-soaps she passed her time with were also not due before 8.30.

Ananya decided to have some fun.

She had often heard her friends chatting, flirting and making friends online.

They said it was fun. They had often urged her to step into the world of VIRTUAL REALITY but Ananya was too time pressed to engage herself in anything like that.

Truth was she felt apprehensive about the whole thing especially after all that she had faced in life.

But this evening was different. Ananya was idle and she wanted company . . . . she wanted to pass time . . . . she wanted some spice in her otherwise busy yet monotonous life.

Ananya sat before her computer,switched it on and connected herself to the internet. She typed her email address . . . . put in her password . . . . and signed in.

The world of *virtual reality* flashed in front of her.

With a fluttering heart Ananya took the cursor to the chat window and clicked on it. A list of **rooms** popped up on the screen.

Ananya clicked on a room where she expected to meet people of her age group. The room was called 'JUST 30'.

A new entrant to this world, Ananya was completely thrown off guard when scores of messages from strange sounding addresses started coming in. There were too many *'hi', 'hello', 'wanna be my friend?', 'lets chat baby', 'asl plz'* . . . . coming in.

Undecided and confused, Ananya ignored all requests and responded to someone who called himself Pushkar. He introduced himself as an IT professional from Bangalore, 34 years of age. He was talking well and Ananya was just beginning to feel comfortable in this strange new world of virtual friends.

But just then it happened . . . . too common in this world . . . . too shocking for Ananya.

Her new found friend asked her, *"don't u feel lonely at nights Ananya?"*

A stunned Ananya remained silent.

The next question swam in," *hey babe, are u hot? What are your vital stats?"*

Anger and disgust had begun to fill her eyes with tears that stung.

She furiously moved the cursor towards the 'sign out' window when suddenly came in a *'hi'* from another stranger.

This was irritating.

She had deliberately kept her status invisible to avoid disturbances, a trick she had heard of from her cyber savvy friends.

Then who was it that had sneaked in?" Must be another of those sex maniacs",thought Ananya bitterly.

By now she was disillusioned about the world of virtual reality.

But strangely, something made her respond. The new comer called himself *'coolsam'*.

Ananya casually typed *'hi Sam'*.

The next question was now expected, *'asl plz'*.

Ananya, with her freshly bitter memories replied, *'yours first plzzzzzz'*.

A *smiley* appeared on her screen as came in the introduction . . . . '33, Male, Guwahati'.

Ananya introduced herself honestly in response.

Coolsam then asked *'can we be friends?'*

Ananya's reply was swift and sharp *'ya but interested only in decent chat. Game?*

Another smiley appeared on Ananya's screen . . . . one showing that the sender was rolling in laughter. Then his reply followed. *'Game. Friends then?'*

Alone in her room Ananya was smiling. *'Yes'* she typed.

She didn't realize her life had just changed.

Samarth, alias 'coolsam', had just cruised into her life as the architect of her new destiny . . .

Chapter 4

"**H**ey what's there in your lunch-box? It smells yummie!"

Ananya was taken aback. It was just the second day of session . . . . a new class . . . . sections shuffled . . . . old friends gone . . . . hardly any familiar face . . . . and now this funny girl coming and asking about the contents of her lunch box . . . . they didn't even know each other!

Ananya felt amused and irritated at the same time. This girl didn't even have the courtesy to say hello or introduce herself. She simply came in asking about her lunch!

"How could people be so shameless?" Ananya wondered. She wouldn't ever imagine doing such a thing with a stranger.

"But this girl sure looks a bully", Ananya thought to herself.

There was however a sweetness about this girl, supposedly a new class mate in the fifth standard, so much so that Ananya couldn't be rude in spite of her irritation.

In any case she could never be rude to anyone however she might dislike that person. So she managed a forced smile.

"Tell na tell na pleasssssssssssssse what is there?"

The desperation in her voice softened Ananya. Her opinion was changing fast.

With her short cropped hair, healthy build and a bubbly look, the girl was more a tomboy than a bully."

"On the whole very cute", decided Ananya, brushing aside her first impression.

"Chicken Chowmin", Ananya replied.

"But there's not much you see . . . . enough for just one", she was quick to add.

It was not everyday that mom made such mouth-watering lunch.

It was actually the left-over of yesterday's dinner, made especially for some guests.

Otherwise cheese sandwich, bread and butter, fruits and similar boring things would fill her lunch box.

So it was not going to be easy to share such rare delicacy.

"That too with someone she doesn't even know the name of?"

"No way!" decided Ananya.

But this girl was so persistent!

"Let me taste a little na pleassssssse. I promise I won't ask for more. My mouth is watering since the time I smelt it and now if I don't taste it I can't concentrate in the class", the girl literally pressed Ananya.

"This is ridiculous!" Ananya thought. And it was not even the first period.

The bell was to go in another minute or so.

But there was something about this girl that touched a cord somewhere in her heart.

Ananya felt an unusual compulsion to relent to her desperate request.

As she hurriedly pulled out the lunch-box which still felt hot, the bell went for the morning assembly.

The next few seconds saw two pairs of little hands working fiercely and then owner of one of them flying towards her own classroom with a thread of noodle still dangling from her mouth and the other laughing her heart out, watching her from the back.

The loss of a part of the special lunch suddenly didn't seem to matter anymore. The sharing was immensely more joyful.

While falling in with the rest of the class for the assembly, Ananya realized that the girl might not even be from her own class and she wondered which class she was in. They didn't even know each other's name. There was hardly time for any conversation.

Strangely, she regretted not having asked. She felt she wanted to meet her again. She wanted them to be friends.

With eyes shut tight, hands clasped, Ananya was religiously repeating the prayer after the Mother Superior when suddenly "ooouch" . . . there was a hard tug at her pony tail.

Angry, startled and scared, lest she should be admonished by the senior prefects for disturbing the prayer session, Ananya only turned to find out who it was. She had a good mind to report the prankster to the teachers after the assembly.

But lo! Who was it looking into her eyes and grinning away happily?

That tomboy . . . who else? And Ananya was flooded with pleasure at this unexpected meeting. It felt like finding back a dear piece of toy after having lost it for sometime.

Looking at the line she was standing in Ananya understood they shared the same class, only she was in a different section. They were both smiling at each other happily, stealing a careful glance at the prefects and the teachers to avoid being reprimanded

For the next four years the disobedient duo became notorious either for talking in the assembly, or for sticking to each other always, or one playing pranks and the other struggling to cover up.

The friendship of Ananya and Katha became a legend in the Marian Convent High School.

One day, at the end of the first month of their friendship, in class five, Ananya and Katha fell out for the first time.

It was a silly issue. Katha had just started spending too much time with another girl from her section.

Ananya, a sentimental fool as she was, started feeling neglected.

She came to know that Katha's new friend was from her locality also and she was a new comer to their school as well.

Katha had taken it upon herself to make the new girl comfortable both in the locality and in the school. Things went a bit too far when she stopped sharing lunch with Ananya for two days at a stretch.

Even an invitation for some mouth-watering 'gajar ka halwa' was turned down. Ananya had forced her mom to make it especially for Katha who cherished a sweet tooth.

On the following day Ananya heaped accusations of disloyalty on her friend, who in turn felt that Ananya was being very selfish.

The result was that they stopped talking to each other.

Their class performance deteriorated, concentration was affected, behaviour with everyone worsened.

It was over a fortnight now that Ananya and Katha were not in talking terms and all their friends were worried. Both the girls were popular in the school for their participation in activities, liveliness and helpful nature.

Everyone was trying in one's own way to help them patch up.

One morning in the recess time, Ananya was sitting alone and sulking when another girl walked in quietly and sat beside her. She remained sitting quietly without intruding into Ananya's thoughts.

She simply remained there.

After a while Ananya felt a little guilty. This girl was her classmate. Her name was Kuhu and she seemed fond of Ananya.

She felt she must talk to her.

Ananya wasn't in a mood to talk so she just smiled at Kuhu, merely acknowledging her presence.

Then Kuhu spoke to her.

She had a very quiet voice, a trifle too matured for a girl of twelve.

"Have patience Ananya, everything will be fine", she said and continued, "If you have such a nice friend like Katha, why do you mind sharing her? Don't you feel proud sharing something nice you have and others don't?

Have faith in your friends."

Very many years after that day, only after streaks of grey had started appearing in her hair, did Ananya realize the meaning and depth of those words.

By that time Kuhu had renounced the material world, joined a mission and become an *ashramite*.

But all through the school life she remained a friend, guide, and philosopher for Ananya.

Though a peer, Ananya looked upon her with esteem and respect.

Her proudest moment was the day she brought Katha and Kuhu together. She wanted all of them to be friends. She wanted to share her prized best friend with the other friend who had taught her the art of sharing and to be proud of the loved ones.

It was just before the annual examinations next year that the three friends learnt that they were not to remain a trio but become quart rets.

This fourth member was an unexpected inclusion in their group. In fact they had all resented it in the beginning.

Sree was never the sort who could have many friends.

There was a haughty air about her which made her a loner.

Usually good looking and fearfully rich girls like Sree, with fantastic academic records, co-curricular achievements and immensely influential fathers, had many admirers but few friends.

But as luck would have it, Ananya, Katha, Kuhu and Sree were put in the same group during the prestigious school exhibition that was held once every three years. They had to do a project on geography—The Natural Resources of India. Making the models for the project was the toughest part of the job. The best project would be selected for a national level inter-school competition.

Katha was a hard working girl but never the serious kind.

Kuhu was honest with her efforts but too detached.

Ananya never had the fire in her belly. She could not nurture ambition because she lacked enough confidence.

It was the ambitious, hardworking, committed and serious natured Sree who changed the lives of the other three during the next one month.

She commanded a kind of involvement from them that none had felt before.

More than for the school, the three friends were putting their life in the project for Sree. They didn't want to let her down. Sree deserved to be a winner and they were prepared to do anything to help her win.

Every time in her life Ananya felt her world disintegrating, her confidence crumbling, her faith shaken, from out of the blue she felt three pairs of hands holding her strongly, whispering words of assurance in her ears, bringing back her faith, her confidence and helping her salvage her pride from the wrecks.

Little had she realized then how the essence of this childhood friendship will stand her in good stead in the years to come.

Chapter 5

Virtual world . . . . Real love
Guwahati
January, 1997

"Samarth?"

Samarth felt a momentary tremor run through him as he looked into her eyes. His gaze was held by a pair of sparkling eyes. She was clad in an ash-black *salwar kameez*, a tea coloured sweater and a white *dupatta* round her neck. She wasn't wearing any make up except a bright lip stick and a mild touch of eye-liner to add prominence to her eyes. Her hair, let loose, was shorter than Samarth had expected. One had to strain one's eyes to detect a spot called *bindi* between her two eye-brows. If there was anything sexy about her, it was indeed, as she had herself claimed her nose-stud. It gave her a kind of north Indian look. She was exactly what she had said she was.

"Yet not a replica of my dream Aan", thought Samarth.

His thought was interrupted.

"Hi Sam!"

Samarth looked again at the extended hand.

Fighting a sudden surge of nervousness, he took it in his own. It was soft and warm. It felt real.

Samarth knew he had camouflaged his nervousness with his characteristic confident smile that hovered on his lips.

But the heart was beating so fast and loud that he feared the person in front might even hear it.

"Hey what's up? *Dumbo*! Want me to spend the rest of the day in the airport?"

She convulsed with laughter.

"A little forced", thought Samarth, "May be she too is fighting to overcome her inhibitions".

The thought made him feel a bit more confident.

"Disappointed Sam?"

Samarth could read the apprehension in the eyes as the question was asked.

He was instantly overpowered by a sudden surge of emotions. Exactly the sort he had been feeling for the last couple of months.

The female standing before him could be best described in just one phrase . . . . 'a child-woman'.

Samarth felt a sudden desperation to enfold her in his arms. She looked so vulnerable. He wanted to protect her.

However this was a public place and Samarth was always careful about keeping emotions bridled, in public places.

But before he could react something strange happened.

She threw herself in his arms and looked up at him.

There were tears welled up in her eyes as she asked innocently, "What happened Sam? You don't love me anymore, isn't it?"

Samarth felt his arms closing about her tightly. His lips brushed her hair. He was least bothered about the people or the place anymore. Everything else seemed to have paled into insignificance. Nothing was real except her.

She was indeed not a replica of his dream girl. But she was Aan. His Aan.

The realization struck and all barriers seemed to melt down.

The excitement and uncertainty of the blind date was over. Reality was sinking in fast.

Samarth and Ananya had set their foot on the real world from the world of virtual.

Little did they know that a love story in the roller-coaster of harsh reality had just been born.

Basking in the tender emotions of their very own virtual world, the world where they had met, Sam and his Aan headed for the hotel.

All through the drive Aan drove him crazy demanding why JC, her *'bhai'*, had not come to receive her.

He had promised to be there even if Samarth failed.

So Ananya went on grumbling with a long face and as the taxi sped towards their destination, Samarth, turning a deaf ear to all her complaints but pretending attention, kept watching her, struggling for composure against an unknown turmoil that had started in him.

He only said to himself, "I love her so much . . . . it pains".

Chapter 6

Farewell Miss Mitra
Durgapur 1976

"Come on girls, lets move towards the auditorium, Miss will be there anytime", Ananya called out to her classmates.

All the girls of the tenth standard stood up quietly in response to the call of their class captain. They had been trying for over the last one week to push away the moment as long as they could.

And now it was there. Time to stand up and face it, a heartrending moment.

Today they queued up in the corridor without the teachers having to yell instructions at them or the prefects monitoring every move of theirs.

Today perfect silence was maintained as they stepped down the stairs and headed for the corridor.

Today not a single head contemplated a prank.

Today the breaths were long.

Today the hearts were heavy.

Today there was a tear in every eye.

Today Miss Mitra was leaving the school for good.

Class x students were now inside the school auditorium. They had taken their seats quietly. The Principal, Vice-principal, Mother Superior, and senior teachers were already up there on the dais. Some of them were busy attending to some last bits of preparations. A big bouquet of colourful flowers stood on the white clothed table. Only they looked very dull today.

All were waiting for the junior teachers to conduct Miss Mitra to her seat on the dais. The wait seemed long and painful.

Ananya had taken her position in the aisle along with her co-prefects.

But she was not there. Her mind drifted back to the days she was in her primary classes and her cousins were in the senior classes in this same school.

The one teacher she had always heard them speaking of fondly was some Miss Mitra, their Vernacular teacher.

As she grew up Ananya gradually got to realize, like every other student in her institution, the kind of influence that this elderly teacher had on the students and on her colleagues.

She was the school's asset not just in terms of her scholarship or professional competence but by sheer virtue of her magic personality. Her very presence made Marian Convent High School, Durgapur such a nice place to be in, a feeling shared unanimously by the students, teachers and all non-teaching staff of the school.

It did not take long for even the naivest of souls to understand that she was an embodiment of professional dedication, motherly affection, friendly support and genuine understanding, not to talk of love, for everyone around her.

Having been a founder member of the school, her long years of dedicated service had so much been taken for granted that none had realized till this day how indispensable she had become for the institution.

Ananya reminiscised how she, along with the other students used to secretly pray in the school chapel, particularly during the dying months of class nine, so that in class x they could be in section A.

Miss Mitra was the class—teacher of class x, section A.

"Good morning Miss", the respectful, emotion-choked chorus shook Ananya out of her reverie.

There she could see in front of her, the slightly stooping, frail structure, clad in a crisply ironed, white-based, cotton printed sari.

With slow poised steps she was making her way towards her seat on the dais, between the principal and the Mother Superior.

The standing ovation, amidst which she exchanged greetings and accepted the bouquet of flowers from the Principal and the school—captain, was expected.

Some formalities were still due. There were mementoes to be presented, speeches to be delivered in recognition of her services and a poem composed by a student to be recited. Together they allowed Ananya enough time to slip back to her reverie again.

Miss Mitra was an angel, a magician, a teacher in the truest sense of the term.

There was not a problem to which she didn't have a solution, not a lesson she failed to make interesting, not a day she hadn't given them a real lesson on life.

What a counselor she was without any formal degree in psychology . . . . she could just read your mind . . . . analyse your problem and offer a solution so simple that you would be left wondering what was so complicated about it after all?

Such was Miss Mitra, a true mentor, for more reasons than one.

Today Miss Mitra was retiring from her thirty year long service career. It was her farewell function that was going on in the school auditorium.

Ananya and her friends had been lucky. Theirs was the last batch taught by Miss Mitra.

Now the moment came that they all had been waiting for with bated breath. It was time for Miss Mitra's parting words, her final address to her students.

Ananya could recollect each and every word that she had spoken on that day.

"Dear students," began her soft, mellow voice, ringing with emotions.

"Let me today tell you before I go, why I have been with you for so many years, why I have been here and not anywhere else?"

There was pin drop silence in the auditorium. Every one listened with rapt attention and interest.

She continued, "I was a small girl then of about seven or eight. My father had taken me to see a play on the Rani of Jhansi. I was very inspired to see that play and secretly decided that one day when I grow up; I would also serve my nation bravely.

As I grew up my debating skills in the school became quite known. My teachers and friends used to advise me to take up law as my subject in future because they felt I would be a very successful lawyer."

She stopped to have a drink of water.

Walking back to the podium she continued, "In college my flair for creative writing was soon noticed by my professors. Suggestions started flowing in that I must take to writing seriously or at least opt for a career in journalism.

Acting on stage however was my passion and I wanted to make my mark in that field. This way my goals and ambitions kept changing.

Towards the end of my academic life I had started feeling very confused. Time was drawing near to choose on some definite career and I felt so indecisive.

I wanted to be so many things all together . . . . but that was not possible.

I spent so many sleepless nights, depressed and morose at the thought of giving up one career for another."

She paused to take a breath.

The entire auditorium was hanging onto her words expectantly. She took off her specks, rubbed them with her handkerchief and put them back again.

"That was the time," she went on, "when one fine morning I decided that I would be a teacher.

Reflecting on all my hidden ambitions of being a lawyer, a journalist, an actor, I realized that the only way I could fulfill all my ambitions was by being a teacher.

Some of my students would become eminent lawyers, some famous actors, some doctors, some engineers, some journalists . . . . the list would be never ending. Through each of them I will live my dreams everyday and live them with pride . . . ."

Her voice was muffled now . . . . the specks were taken off to let the tears flow . . . . She held the microphone strongly with both hands as if to steady herself.

The silence was deafening.

Each second seemed like a year . . . till the teachers on the dais put their hands together for their devoted colleague.

Within moments they were joined by the students and the entire remaining staff who had been listening so long, mesmerized.

As the thundering applause strove to drown the silent tears streaming down so many eyes, one girl standing in the aisle with rapt attention so long had just realized what her aim in life was.

Ananya was going to be a teacher . . . . a teacher like Miss Mitra!

Chapter 7

In The Jaws of Hell
Kolkata
1984

Ananya stopped for a while and turned back. He was nowhere in sight. Her heart was beating too loudly.

"I can't be nervous, I got to move on, we can't afford to lose this chance, I have to save him", Ananya kept muttering to herself with every step she took forward.

The narrow street she had been walking along had culminated in a still narrower lane.

"Am I on the right path?" she wondered for a while. But the other lane was a blind one; she could make that out from here itself. So she must be on the right track.

Ananya kept walking in short, hesitant steps. The lane was dark and dingy. It stank so severely of urine and rotten vegetables that she was scared she might throw up.

"What is the time?" she wondered. They had come out of the house in such a hurry that she had forgotten her watch. The look of the place did not suggest that sunlight got to reach here even in the day time.

The narrow street she had been walking on, a while back, was lined with straggling slums on both sides. This lane however was deserted. It seemed to serve as the bathroom and dustbin for the slum dwellers. Except for a few urchins playing and fighting among themselves, Ananya did not notice anyone.

One of them shot her a curious glance, certainly surprised at the sight of someone like her, a complete mismatch with the surroundings. But he too soon busied himself in the snatch and run game with his friends.

"Is this place in Kolkata?" Ananya couldn't help wondering.

They were given an address on the Free School Street but this place seemed so cut off from the civilized world that it could not possibly have any address. It was difficult to believe that only about five to seven minutes back she had been standing on one of the busiest and poshest thoroughfares of the city and now suddenly she was alone in a shady, semi-deserted, narrow, stinking alley.

She had barely walked for another five minutes when suddenly she stopped. She could see it in front of her. It was just a few steps away.

The building was old but imposing. The yellow paint on the exterior seemed peeled off long ago. Moss and damp covered most part of the shabby, cracked walls. What however arrested Ananya's attention was the huge wooden door almost royal and palatial in appearance. With its intricate carvings, exquisite in spite of the thick dust cover, this door, much like the last remains of a historical wreck, somehow seemed a complete contrast to the rest of the building.

From the look of the lane it was difficult to guess that a building like this was standing at the end of it. It loomed up so suddenly that she was a little taken aback.

Ananya moved up to the door with brisk, nervous steps. She looked around. There was no one in sight. The three storied building hardly looked inhabited.

"Where am I to knock?" she thought. There was neither any door knob nor any bell and it was not possible to bang on this huge, hard, solid wooden door.

Ananya stood there a while, baffled; and then before she had actually done anything, the door before her opened with a creak giving her a start. Somebody from the other side was coming out. Ananya heard few snatches of some rapid conversation, "Urdu perhaps", she thought.

She couldn't follow any of it, didn't even bother also. She was too nervous and too preoccupied with her own problem.

The men who emerged from behind the giant door looked typical *pathans,* those commonly known in kolkata lingo as *kabuliwallahs.* Ananya had seen them from a distance earlier. She had heard stories about them. The stories did not match her first impressions of the *kabuliwallah* she had read about in Tagore's renowned collection of short stories when she was thirteen.

She had heard that these people were ruthless money lenders who lent out money at cut-throat rate of interest and resorted to violence if the loan or the interest was not paid on time. They were a dreaded lot because of the scene they created, abuses they hurled and threats they pronounced to the defaulters, publicly. Decent people, at least the peace loving self respectful ones were known to maintain their distance from this lot unless misfortune drove them to a situation desperate enough to pile at the doorstep of these *kabuliwallahs.*

Ananya was one of those unfortunate ones.

The two middle-aged, bearded men in front of her were dressed in grey colored *sherwanis* with faded black turbans wound about their heads. The beard covered the best parts of their chest.

They threw a curious glance at Ananya, clearly surprised.

Ananya could sense that women were not expected visitors in these places, more so unaccompanied women.

They had stopped conversing at the sight of Ananya.

The silence that momentarily fell between them was uncomfortable.

Ananya, nervous as she was, attempted a conversation, "*khan saab yehin rehte hai kya?*" Does Khan Saab stay here?

They hesitated a moment before replying and then said in their typical accented hindi, "*wei idaar tu bhout kaan ayi, aapku kon chaiye?*" There are many Khans here, who are you asking for?

Ananya was not prepared for this. She tried to recollect if Sayan had ever mentioned any first name of the khan but nothing struck.

"*aap andar jaake deko*", Go inside and find out, was all they said before leaving.

Ananya was thankful to them at least for pushing open the door for her. Though the men looked curious they did not ask her many questions. Ananya felt they were in a hurry. While stepping inside the house with a trepidating heart Ananya had a feeling that those men had turned back to look at her. But she did not turn round to check.

Ananya found herself stepping onto a wide cemented courtyard, partly in the darkness of the lengthening shadow and partly wearing the soft pink glow of the setting sun. There were five clotheslines at the sunny end of the rectangular courtyard from which dozens of sherwanis of various colours were hanging, evidently left to be dried after wash.

Ananya noticed there was not a single piece of any female garment. It was a men's world, she realized and the thought sent a quick chill down her spine. But this was no time for such fear. Considering Sayan's present situation she couldn't afford it.

Ananya crossed the courtyard quickly and found herself in front of another wooden door, a less formidable one this time.

Luckily this one was not shut. Probably the men she met outside had left it partly open.

Breathing a quick prayer Ananya pushed the door open and stepped inside. The sight in front of her left her gaping. She found herself standing in a huge hall with a discolored, old stretch of floor mat covering the length of it from wall to wall. Here and there the cement floor peeped from underneath the torn points of the mat. The walls were damp and cracked in most places. Some parts of the wall were stained with beetle spit.

Ananya noticed that the far end of the hall was dominated by a long low table covered with a white cloth. The table was full of containers filled with food items. The place smelled sharply of onion, garlic, spices and cooked meat. At least fifty people were seated at the table and another nearly thirty were waiting to join them.

They were folding up their rags evidently after finishing their evening namaz *Maghrib*.

The near end of the hall was occupied by a dozen elderly men. Few of them were engaged in conversation, another few were seemingly getting ready to sleep.

"How am I to find the one I am looking for?" Ananya wondered.

She noticed a couple of young men; apparently in their late thirties busy talking to one pathan. It seemed they were asking for a loan but the lender was not too sure about their credibility.

Ananya knew they insisted on having somebody to stand a guarantee for the borrower and also went for a physical verification of the residence before they gave the money.

Sayan had given her a name to quote as reference, some Belal from Tollygunge. The fellow had even sent a phone number in case they wanted to talk to him before granting the loan to her.

The room was filled with noise and smell. Nervous as she already was, Ananya felt nausea tic.

She decided to approach one of the elderly men to ask for the specific Khan she was looking for.

She had barely taken a step forward when she froze where she was.

A dead silence had suddenly settled in the hall.

With every noise quietened, only the strong smell of the cooked meat hung heavily in the air.

Ananya sensed that every pair of eye present in the room had turned to her. Over hundred men, all strangers, in a god forsaken place were holding her with their gaze. It was a moment Ananya was not going to forget for the rest of her life.

She stood motionless where she was.

The words of one elderly pathan broke the silence that had suddenly settled from nowhere.

"*Koun chaiye?*" he asked in accented hindi.

Ananya was acutely aware of everybody's attention focused on her.

Even the two young men haggling for their own loan had fixed their surprised gaze on Ananya. A woman was the least expected presence in a place like this.

"Khan saab", she managed somehow and then expecting the next question she hurriedly added, *"Naam nehi pata, Belal bheja hai"*.

The mention of Belal had probably struck a chord somewhere for the man now asked, *"Kya kaam hai kaan se?Paisa chaiye?"* There was a strange ridicule in his voice and Ananya felt her ears burning.

But she had no time for such things; she needed to see the man she had come for. Sayan's hopes were pinned on her. The very thought of failing to get the money and the consequences of it sent a shudder through her.

She nodded in response to the question. By now buzzes and peals of laughter had filled the room.

From the far end of the hall two younger men came walking towards her and flashed a mocking smile exposing ugly, stained teeth. *"Akeli ayi ho?"* one of them asked.

Ananya could do little but nod. *"Paisa chaiye?"* the other one said.

Ananya could hear the laughter rising all around her.

She could not follow any bit of the conversations going on around her but stood there surrounded by innumerable indecent men, unaware of their intentions.

If a dirty gaze could strip a woman, Ananya felt stripped of her dignity. She was fighting fear and tears simultaneously.

She had no idea what these men wanted from her but the way they looked at her from head to toe and jeered, Ananya felt worse than molested. Their lusty, teasing glance running through her body was no worse than being actually touched by them.

The stares cut through her flesh. Ananya felt raped, torn, ripped apart. Insult and humiliation were threatening to overpower her any moment.

The ugly gestures they made filled her with anger and shame.

No one looked friendly in that place. For them it was clearly a novel experience to have a woman coming alone to them asking for money.

Most certainly they had sensed her need and desperation and were extracting their own share of fun out of it.

Ananya was literally scared now. She had forgotten the purpose of her visit. She was only thinking of escape from this place. The collective laughter around her was driving her crazy.

Pushing away the thought of the terrible consequences if she returned from here empty handed, Ananya turned back to face the door.

"What do I tell Sayan? What will happen to him?"

"Paisa nehi chaiye?" The words along with a fresh peal of laughter pierced Ananya from the back.

She did not turn to look. All her instincts pushed her towards the door and out of it.

She ran across the courtyard, running into one clothesline. Some of the clothes fell from the line.

Ananya was least bothered. Tears stung her eyes painfully. She could hardly see.

Somehow she reached the giant door and pushed it with all her might. It opened more easily than she had expected.

With her heart beating in her throat Ananya stepped out in the open. She felt grateful as the darkness instantly wrapped her in a close embrace.

Ananya was not scared of the dark. It was in fact a relief to be hidden in its arms.

She walked ahead as though in a trance, blind to everything ahead of her and just walked on as fast as her legs could carry her as far as possible from the hell she had just been to.

She groped for her way along the lane at the end of which she knew sayan would be waiting expectantly for her . . . . and along with him would wait a new hell.

Chapter 8

Disillusioned
Shillong
January 1, 1997

Samarth didn't want to disturb her. She seemed to be sleeping very peacefully.

Looking at the innocent sleeping face, comfortably resting against his bare chest, he was suddenly swept over by a rush of tenderness for this girl.

"She looks so vulnerable, so helpless", Samarth thought.

He suddenly wanted to hold her close, very close to himself and protect her from the world that had been so brutal to her. But he allowed sense to rule over sensibility.

No he couldn't allow himself to get carried away anymore. He had already made a serious damage which could not be mended.

He couldn't risk anymore mistake now.

So Samarth chose to remain motionless as Ananya slept, curled up against him, completely at peace, unaware that her dream world had come crashing down even before she could think of making it a reality.

It was almost 9.30 as Samarth checked the time on his cell phone.

Fortunately it was Saturday and he didn't need to rush to office.

But he was swept over by a secret feeling of guilt as he wished desperately that it was a normal working day instead of his weekly day-off.

The office which seemed so appalling on other mornings, suddenly felt like a haven of refuge.

"Am I trying to avoid facing Ananya?" Samarth wondered.

A fresh feeling of self-disgust filled him from head to toe.

He tried stealing a glance at Ananya, blissfully unaware of the turbulence going on within him.

But something stopped him. A mixed feeling of guilt, disgust and regret made him feel sick. He wanted to rush to the bathroom and throw up but couldn't move an inch.

Ananya was clinging on to his bare flesh with both hands. There was a strange plea for love and protection in her closed eyes, a desperate need for dependence in the way she clutched at him. And Samarth remained glued to his position.

Almost an hour later Ananya woke up happily in his arms and proceeded cheerfully to the bathroom to freshen up and get ready for the first day of her life with Samarth, on the first day of a fresh, new, year. She was thrilled.

Released from her hold, Samarth walked towards the window, as though in a trance. He opened the curtains. The morning outside was bright and sunny. But to Samarth there was only darkness around.

The sun had blinded him.

"How am I looking Sam?"

Samarth was jerked back to senses as he turned to face Ananya.

Dressed in blue jeans and light yellow kurta top with simple matching ear studs and a pendent hanging from her neck, Ananya was smiling at him expectantly.

"What am I supposed to say?" Samarth wondered.

Her bare body in the night before came before his eyes in a flash.

Samarth pushed away the memory guiltily.

The flames of passion had been doused off by reality. What remained were only the ashes of disappointment.

"How do I tell you that the flab around your waistline is ugly?

That the funky designer rings round your fingers do not make up for your thinning hairline?

That your sexy nose stud does not make you the least youthful at 34?"

Crumbling under the pressure of guilt Samarth wanted to cry out, *"you are not the Ananya I had imagined you to be from our chat sessions! You are the biggest disappointment of my life.*

I had agreed on a blind date with a different image in my mind, I tried my best to accept you but I can't, I can't, I can't.

Oh God! Ananya forgive me but you are not the one I was waiting for . . . ."

"Samarth, I am asking you something", Ananya cried out again impatiently.

Samarth only heard himself say, "you are looking great my dear. Now lets not waste anymore time. JC will be waiting for us in Guwahati."

Samarth literally dashed inside the bathroom to have his bath and get ready.

It was a welcome relief for sometime.

He just couldn't bear to face her anymore.

Her eyes were full of trust and love for him and Samarth found it unbearable.

He could never bring himself to hurt this woman; not after all that she had already gone through in life.

"No, I will only fill her life with happiness even at the cost of my dreams", Samarth resolved as the warm water ran all over him.

But even the resolution did not pacify the turbulence within him.

Toweling himself dry he went on debating with himself, "won't that be cheating? What has Ananya done to deserve this hypocrisy?"

The questions made his head spin. He couldn't think any more.

So brushing aside the disturbing thoughts for the time being, Samarth concentrated on dressing up.

All through he was aware of being pierced by Ananya's glance as he slipped into a pair of stonewashed trousers, and a blue Monte Carlo pullover that Ananya had brought for him.

The two then set out to begin the first day of the first year of their life.

A happy, exuberant Ananya, her hands locked with that of a disturbed, confused Samarth.

Chapter 9

Sayan—the darkness
Shillong
January,1997

As the indigo blue Wagon-R snaked down the Shillong Mountains, Ananya felt her stomach churn a little.

It was the winding descent that she was not used to.

The morning was beautiful and nature was at her best.

Always passionate about long drives, what more could she have asked for than driving down a breathtaking hilly tract on a pleasant sunny morning with none other than Samarth beside her?

But this churning in the stomach was spoiling the fun.

The last thing she wanted was to fall sick and waste away the day.

So deciding against taking that kind of risk, Ananya took out an *avomin* which she always carried in her purse for emergency situations like this.

She gulped down the small blue tablet quickly before Samarth could notice and ask questions.

After all it was nothing so serious that she needed Samarth to bother with.

But she knew she would soon doze off to an uncontrollable sleep. That was the only disturbing effect of this medicine.

Samarth was unusually silent.

"Is anything wrong?" suddenly Ananya wondered. "Is he disturbed for some reason or am I imagining too much?"

However she chose not to ask anything. If something was wrong, Samarth would surely tell her.

Hardly had such fleeting thoughts died down when Ananya's eyes started feeling heavy. The churning in the stomach was gradually giving way to a rather imposing sleep as she had expected.

Ananya knew she wouldn't be able to keep her eyes open for long. She wanted to coze up in Samarth's arms wishing he had his arm round her.

But Samarth was at the far end of the seat and seemed to be lost in his own world of thoughts.

So Ananya shifted slightly and quietly towards him and rested her head lightly on his shoulder.

Samarth turned to her. He looked worried.

"Are you okay? Any problem?"

The concern in his voice touched Ananya.

"I am fine Sam, just a little sleepy . . . . Over exertion of last night I guess", She giggled.

Samarth laughed back in full agreement.

There was a youthful spirit in her which appealed to Samarth.

He was not even aware when his right arm had already gone around Ananya holding her in a strong, protective grip.

Samarth actually felt nice about it.

His own reaction surprised him.

For Ananya it was all a new experience. First time ever, after her father, she was enjoying the love and protection of a man.

Seven years back she thought she was not destined to enjoy all this and her world was engulfed in an impenetrable darkness.

Ananya's mind drifted back to a winter morning in the year 1999.

The day was 19th of December. She had left her bed in the morning tensed and heavy-headed.

All through the previous night she had been busy talking to Sayan.

It was so difficult to convince him for marriage. Their courtship had just completed a year and Ananya's parents insisted that they settle down without delay.

She was already 27 and her parents were too middle class tempered to allow prolonging it.

So their condition was simple and blunt.

Either marry and settle down immediately or stop dating and wait quietly till both were ready to tie the knot.

But how could Ananya tell her parents that Sayan had not yet spoken to his family about her?

The revelation would adversely affect Sayan's image before them. They might even suspect his intentions.

No, she couldn't let that happen.

Sayan was a nice person, extremely handsome, working in a forth ranking MNC, earning well, commanding a charming personality . . . . most importantly in love with her.

As far as Ananya's feelings were concerned, she was head over heels in love with him. She enjoyed the jealous glances of the ladies piercing her when she walked on the streets with Sayan.

No she couldn't afford to lose Sayan at any cost.

True, there were some disturbing abnormalities about him but Ananya chose to ignore it all.

Sayan had finally agreed to a court-marriage and that was enough for the time being. So what if there was something uncanny about it with Sayan stubbornly refusing to inform family or friends about the marriage?

Ananya decided to bury these questions for the time being.

After all so many marriages took place secretly without parental consent but with time everything fell into place.

Poor Sayan was already compromising so much for her just because he loved her so much, couldn't she be a little more patient? And if he was only asking for a little more time to break the news at home, what was wrong with that?

Sayan had already told her how strict his parents were and how much his father was forcing him to marry his friend's daughter.

Ananya couldn't help nurturing a bitterness for her would-be in-laws who, she learnt from Sayan valued money and status above everything else.

Unfortunately Ananya's family had none of these and so it was quite likely that they would oppose their elder son's decision to marry her.

She however kept her thoughts focused on Sayan who alone mattered to him.

Expect for one or two issues that had roused some doubts in her heart', Sayan had been an exciting boyfriend.

On a few occasions Sayan had sneaked into her house at very late hours of night, jumping over the boundary wall, asking for money.

But he always had convincing reasons to wipe off even the slightest doubt in her heart. Sometimes he would say how he was desperately trying to help out a friend in distress whereas at other times he would simply say that his brother was in some kind of emergency and unfortunately he had left his purse in the office and so the only one he could think of turning to for help was Ananya. And Ananya would only feel too obliged to help.

Had it not been for Sayan she would never have known what it meant to be blindly in love.

There was just one habit of Sayan, which Ananya found very embarrassing, particularly in front of her parents.

He always needed to use the toilet whenever he dropped in at her place. He never left the toilet before at least an hour.

The frowns on her parents' face made her feel all the more uncomfortable.

But Sayan, far from being apologetic would casually explain that it was a case of stomach disorder.

Of course Ananya never bothered to find out why he suffered from upset stomach so frequently.

It did not strike Ananya even once that the day they had chosen to get their marriage registered quietly was a Sunday and Government offices were supposed to remain closed on Sundays.

She anyway didn't need to bother when Sayan was there to take care of it all.

That afternoon Ananya faithfully followed Sayan Dasgupta into the interior of a spooky looking office in central Kolkata and in the presence of a most unconvincing looking bearded man, signed on a piece of paper along with Sayan and was told that from that day she was Mrs.Ananya Dasgupta, the legally wedded wife of Mr.Sayan Dasgupta.

Even before she could feel the excitement of it all, her marriage was over without the presence of a family member or a friend, without music, without the conventional bridal make—up, without any sound of cheer or laughter, not even a pinch of *sindoor* to give her the feel of being married.

Sayan maintained a stoical silence during those five minutes and then hastily called a taxi.

Before Ananya could say or ask anything, the driver was directed to take her home. Alone.

He said he would be following her soon after wrapping up some urgent work.

The legal document of marriage that had been promised by the bearded man within a week of the signing ritual, never reached her.

The news of the secret court—marriage quite expectedly earned the ire of both families. The newly—wed couple was sternly told to fend for their own.

However Ananya's parents were comfortable about the marriage. What upset them was the indifference of Sayan's family.

In spite of all the odds, Ananya was excited the day they shifted to a rented apartment.

It was just two days after her marriage. They were to be the tenants of Sayan's friend who lived in the first floor of a luxurious house and was letting out the ground floor that was semi furnished too.

Ananya had loved the house at first sight.

She was confident that she would do up the place nicely in course of time. It would be their first home, the nest of two love-birds.

She silently promised herself that she would be the best possible wife and fill Sayan's life with happiness. She was grateful for all the compromises that Sayan had made for her.

Little could Ananya sense that misfortune was waiting with open, avid jaws to devour her very soon.

It was their first night together.

So what if the night had nothing in common with the dreams that she had cherished like every other girl? It was still her wedding night.

Devoid of bridal fineries and jewellery, Ananya still waited with a fluttering, heart to surrender her womanhood to the man she loved and become united with him in body and soul.

The husband never came.

The bride kept waiting in shock, horror and dismay.

Sayan did not touch Ananya for the next seven months.

The marriage was not consummated.

But Ananya carefully guarded the secret. She couldn't let this relationship down before anyone, particularly Sayan's parents who she knew would only be too happy to learn that things were not running well between them.

She will die but she won't give in. And who knows things might change for the better in future.

No one however knew better than Ananya that nothing would change.

She was doomed forever.

Within a week of their marriage Ananya had found out that Sayan was severely addicted to drugs.

To make matters worse he was an infidel. He had conned her into marriage to get hold of some jewelry that his wife would bring along and clear up the debt that he had incurred while procuring drugs.

He was never serious about the affair and would have ditched her anyway but the pressure from the creditors had forced him into this marriage.

Having got hold of the jewellery that Ananya's mother had given her, he sold them off to clear off some of his pending debts.

Now he didn't need her any longer except to earn and maintain that household because he had no place to go.

His family had disowned him already.

Sayan kept losing one job after another. His addiction was easily discovered everywhere due to the growing abnormalities in his behaviour.

On top of that he was irregular, a compulsive liar and a fraud who was always cheating on credit cards or forging papers just to raise money for drugs.

During the next three years Sayan went on incurring loans at high interests and Ananya went on working harder and harder to meet the increasing financial demands.

Sayan still managed to work but contributed nothing to the family.

Ananya was a most unwelcome piece of existence in his life and he chose to live with his former live-in partner Obja.

It was long since Ananya had stopped crying.

There were just two regrets she couldn't come to terms with.

The first was the pain she would cause to her parents if her marriage broke and secondly for never getting the chance to be a mother.

She loved children.

But Ananya was a fighter. She fought relentlessly and single handed to make things better, at least workable.

She tried to get Sayan treated and even took care of him like a child every time he writhed in pains of withdrawal in front of her.

Deep down in her heart however Ananya knew that she was fighting a lost battle.

But everything has to end someday.

Ananya's patience and tolerance broke down the day Sayan eloped with the neighbour's daughter leaving behind a note that he would never return again.

That night Ananya returned to her parents' home . . . with all her faith shattered, confidence broken, burden of huge loans on her shoulders and on the verge of a nervous breakdown.

On the 1$^{st of}$ November,1987, almost after two and a half years of being married, Ananya, her father's darling, buried her face in his chest and cried.

Holding his daughter tightly, a helpless father felt his whole world getting flooded away before his eyes

As the car screeched to a halt, Ananya sat up. Her eyes still heavy.

"Have we reached Samarth?" She asked.

"Yes", Samarth replied. "You wait in the car and let me go and see where JC is waiting."

Samarth went towards a coffee shop where JC was supposed to be waiting.

Ananya eagerly looked forward to meet the man who had become more than a brother to him though they had never met before and had only spoken on the phone.

Chapter 10

Goodbye Samarth
Shillong
January, 1997

Ananya was almost in tears when JC enfolded her in a big bear hug and chirped, *"Hi sister"*.

There was a strange affection in his voice which instantly told Ananya that this was the brother who she had awaited all her life.

"This is not a stranger I am meeting for the first time".

She felt an instant bond with this fair, cute, six feet man with a shy smile and she knew this was the brother figure she had always missed since her childhood.

To herself Ananya said silently, "thank you Samarth for this wonderful gift."

During the next four days Ananya experienced heaven.

In this new city she experienced love for the first time in the form of Samarth and got a brother like JC.

"Thank you God", she said to herself again and again.

But fortunately or unfortunately for Ananya, she was a very sensitive individual with a very sharp insight.

She perceived things which nobody expected or wanted her to. But most often she kept her perceptions to herself while her heart bled silently.

Samarth was a fantastic man. He was the kind of man Ananya had always dreamt of spending her life with.

He didn't have the flashy looks of Sayan and at times even lacked finesse in certain issues.

But there was softness about him, a tender heart with immense feelings for everyone around him, which touched Ananya's heart.

Almost all the nights they were together Ananya could hear him at sometime or the other grumbling to himself affectionately, "this girl can't even keep her blanket on properly" and he would tuck her up carefully just the way dad used to do when she was a child and kicked off the blanket while sleeping.

"Old habits die hard", she would chuckle when Samarth told her the next morning how she had her leg on his waist all through the night or tugged at his blanket after throwing off her own.

He was a kind of man one couldn't help loving.

Sometimes he was too blunt with his observations and comments on people and situations but there again he had that unmistakable quality of honesty which demanded admiration.

Samarth was not a man who could talk to please and this Ananya had readily understood.

He expected the same of the people around him.

Yes, he did hurt sometimes with his remarks but then again he never did so intentionally. It's just that it was his nature to call a spade, a spade.

Samarth's blunt honesty made Ananya love him all the more.

Having lived with an imposter like Sayan, she had for a long time forgotten to trust people.

It seemed everybody talked to impress, everybody seemed to be play acting, and everybody seemed to try to be what they were not.

The world scared Ananya till the time she met Samarth.

His simplicity charmed her and his open hearted communication made her love him and trust him very easily.

It was Samarth who had brought Ananya's faith back in life and she wanted to live the rest of her life with him.

Once again Ananya felt that life is beautiful.

Samarth was indeed like a surge of fresh air after the stifling life she had with Sayan.

I want to fill your life with happiness", she kept telling herself.

Those were fun—filled four days for the trio.

Ananya, Samarth and JC had the best time of their life during those four days.

In spite of rigorous work schedule the men stole time to take Ananya round the city, they ate together, shopped together, went places together and above all laughed together.

Samarth literally forgot his own initial disappointments and JC only watched with amusement how Samarth's feelings about Ananya as he had disclosed to him in the coffee shop and his real actions were contradicting each other.

"Sam, are you sure buddy you know your heart too well?" JC kept wondering more and more.

They had been friends for over two decades now and never before had he seen so much disparity between Samarth's words and actions.

"I must counsel him before he makes any mistake. He doesn't realize he is in love with this woman, he mustn't let her go" he would tell himself repeatedly the more he saw them together.

To Ananya he would say in Samarth's absence, "Don't judge him by his exterior sis. He's a great guy".

Of course Ananya had no doubt about it herself.

"But there are things you won't understand bro, you are too simple to understand all that", she would think. However apparently she would only nod her head agreement.

The four days literally flew past.

Finally the morning came when Ananya had to return.

Her flight was at 3.30 in the afternoon and Samarth had a press conference to attend at 1.30. So it was decided that JC would see Ananya off at the airport.

Samarth was full of genuine regret for his inability to accompany Ananya to the airport. His eyes were moist when he hugged her tightly and whispered in her ears, "I am sorry Aan, I hate myself for this", but Ananya felt secretly thankful.

She knew she would break down during the final parting moments and she didn't want to create a scene in the public.

She too hated public display of private emotions.

Ananya had struggled to maintain her calm all through the morning.

There was a different storm blowing through her mind.

Samarth was irritated with himself. He always felt in this way whenever he failed to analyse anything logically. The day he had cast the first look on Ananya, he knew this was not the woman he had imagined or expected to meet and yet why was he feeling so morose about Ananya's leaving.

Samarth felt he would go mad.

"Why don't I want Ananya to leave? Why do I wish her to stay back?" were the questions gnawing at his heart. "No I am not in love with her and this I know for sure."

"Then what is it?" The more he tried to force an answer out of himself the more frustrated he felt. He wanted to get rid of Ananya and keep her at the same time.

The dilemma was unbearable.

Samarth and Ananya hardly spoke that morning.

They both seemed to share a common feeling . . . if the worst has to happen, let it happen . . . if they have to part they should part without delay.

But even through their silence they spoke volumes to each other . . . very much the way they sometimes did over the phone.

There had been days when for long long stretches of time the two had simply held on to the phone feeling each other's breath in complete silence.

When just about ten minutes were left for Samarth to leave, Ananya finally broke the brooding silence.

"Thanks Sam, Thanks for everything".

"Hey come on Ananya", Samarth protested in genuine embarrassment. "What's this formality for? We both had a great time."

He was surprised to find his voice choke while talking.

Ananya walked to the sofa and sat beside him. For the last four days they had been living together in this hotel room on most intimate terms and yet suddenly this distance between the bed where she was sitting so long and the sofa where Samarth was, seemed unbridgeable.

But Ananya knew that time had come for her to act.

"I must speak up now", she prepared herself. The moment that she had been dreading had finally come.

She must tell Samarth about it and this couldn't be done over the phone.

She had to muster all her courage. It was difficult but not impossible.

"Sam", Ananya touched his hand carefully. Samarth looked at her.

First time in the course of the last four days he couldn't read the expression in her eyes.

But there was something there that made him very uncomfortable. His apprehensions were rising.

"Goodbye Sam".

The voice seemed to float in from very far away.

He tried to force a laugh.

In his characteristic blunt manner he heard himself saying, "oh come on sweetheart, you needn't be so melodramatic. We are going to meet soon . . . . depending on my leave availability you see . . ."

The words seemed to hurry out of his mouth before he could even choose them correctly.

"No Samarth, we will never meet again".

The cool seriousness in her voice chilled him.

"Why Ananya?" He found himself shocked.

A sad smile rested on Ananya's lips.

"Ask yourself Sam", she said softly.

"I am not the woman of your dreams darling, and I can't ruin the dreams of the man I love".

"Nonsense", Samarth tried to protest.

This girl had read his mind. He felt awkwardly exposed.

"But who on earth gave you such an idea?" he still fought to defend himself.

This time Ananya steeled herself.

"Nobody needed to tell me anything Sam. Your inherent honesty makes you too transparent."

Time was running out. Even if he wished he couldn't stay back to explain anything. It was the Chief Minister's press meet and he had to attend. In fact he was already late. Ananya had chosen a very wrong time for the discussion.

No, but he had to stop her. He couldn't let her go away like that. They had together made this relationship possible, now she couldn't pronounce her verdict single handedly like that.

Samarth felt desperate.

As he rushed towards the door, he only shouted back helplessly, "we'll talk it out on phone Ananya, I'll explain . . . ." his voice died down.

As the elevator carried him down from the fifth floor of the hotel, Samarth felt his whole world was tumbling down with every moment of descent.

Suddenly he felt a desperate urge to run back to her. He wanted to hold her and cry. An incomprehensible sense of loss gripped him.

Tears stung his eyes and the world blurred before him.

Chapter 11

They are the world . . . . they are the children

Rrrring . . . rr . . . rring . . . the telephone bell almost made Samarth jump to his feet.

Ever since he had returned to office from the press conference, he was lost in his own world of thoughts. It was difficult to concentrate in work today.

Ananya seemed to have taken away his soul with her.

Rrrrrrring . . . rrring . . . . rring . . .

"This damned phone will never stop ringing", Samarth cursed.

"Hello", he said, the irritation clearly reflected in his voice.

"Hello Sam, its JC here".

"Oh hi, tell me. Was she alright?" The concern spilled over his words spontaneously.

"Yeah she was fine. I thought I found her eyes a bit watery . . . I may be wrong you see", JC replied.

"Hunnn", a deep sigh was all Samarth could let out.

"Sister has left a note for you. When can you collect it?"

"Why? You aren't coming down this side?" Samarth asked, impatient.

"No *yaar*, sorry, I am a bit tied up today. You can take it tomorrow or come over and collect it from my office. In any case it doesn't matter anymore . . . does it Sam?"

"It does yaar, it does", Samarth wanted to cry but all he heard himself say was, "yeah it doesn't matter anymore".

On the other end of the line JC was little convinced.

As he replaced the receiver he smiled quietly, "If I know you well enough dear friend then this note will be collected before the end of the day"

It was 5.30 pm when Ananya's flight touched down. It had been delayed by 15 minutes. She had tried to keep herself busy through the last couple of hours trying to plan out the rigorous work schedule that lay ahead.

After collecting her luggage from the conveyor belt, Ananya pushed her trolley towards the exit looking for her driver. She had already spoken to him over the phone and he had confirmed that he would be there.

"Mommm", a familiar voice pierced her ears.

Ananya swung her neck and was swept over by a pleasant surprise.

She was looking into two brightly lit up faces . . . flushed with the unmistakable joy of meeting her.

Siddharth and Vivek had come to receive her.

"We decided to surprise you", Vivek smiled as he took charge of the trolley.

"We knew your car would be waiting but still we thought you would like to see us instead of the driver", Siddharth winked innocently.

"I am so happy", Ananya beamed in genuine joy and hugged the duo warmly.

"You know mom our New Year is yet to begin", chirped Siddharth.

"It couldn't possibly have without you", said Vivek in agreement.

As Ananya's wine red Santro Xing sped towards her Behala residence from the Kolkata airport, the two boys poured out their celebration plans.

Ananya was told the party had been postponed for her and they were all awaiting her return eagerly. She felt overwhelmed.

"Ok tell me when are we having our New Year bash? I guess we are already late by four days!"

Ananya tried to sound enthusiastic to match their spirits.

"And how many of you will be there?" she asked.

"Oh mom! What a question!" Siddharth sounded slightly exasperated.

"The usual dozen of course", quipped Vivek.

"Has it ever been otherwise? Why'd you still need to ask mom?" Siddharth sounded hurt.

"Tonight you rest and tomorrow we'll have the party in our terrace", he added.

"You know mom, his father has made fantastic arrangements for us . . . I mean the feast and the lights" Vivek said excitedly.

"Music of course we will organize to suit our taste", Siddharth reminded.

"Really?" Ananya responded with genuine interest this time.

"Then I am not sure I can patiently wait through tonight even", she threw back her head and laughed and the boys joined in.

These boys had been Ananya's students since they were in the fourth standard. Now they were in Standard twelve.

Neither Ananya nor they had realized since when she had become their best friend and eventually their mother.

'mom' had long since replaced *'maam'* and the change had been gradual and natural.

Theirs was a group of twelve, nine boys and three girls.

They were Ananya's children. They comprised her world.

True, she loved all her students equally well but this special *'dozen'*, made Ananya feel the essence of motherhood.

They trusted her with every detail of their experiences of growing up, confided in her the subtlest of their emotions, and intensely.

They were God's greatest gift to her. They sustained her when she was going through the trauma of a broken marriage, they made her laugh amidst gloom and they silently seemed to remind her always, "you are not alone mom, we are always there".

The children were Ananya's assets. It wasn't enough to say that she was proud of them. She taught them, partied with them, went for movies and drives with them, scolded them when they strayed, counseled them whenever necessary, laughed and cried with them.

"Even today they are here, as though god-sent, when I need them so much. Indeed my New Year has also not started, how could it without my children?"

Suddenly she felt a surge of relief. Thank God she was back.

Back to her world. The world of these children, the world to which she belonged.

"Thank You Miss Mitra, without your example to follow this wouldn't have been possible. Thank you for helping me to be the kind of teacher I had always wanted. Thank you for helping me to be like you. Otherwise I would never have had the love of these children." Ananya kept uttering to herself silently and gratefully.

Far away in the city of Guwahati, in a lonely corner of his room Samarth was reading a note which said,

Dear Sam,

Sorry I couldn't fulfill your dream. Thanks again and again for being such a nice friend. Try to forget me if you can as I will too. And please don't call or mail. It would only make things difficult for both of us. We both have our purposes in life and let's try and do justice to those. Don't feel bad for anything. It's all a part of life. Wish you all the very best in life. God bless you.

Yours ever
Ananya

Chat room–just30s

With tears streaming down his eyes, Samarth felt his world crushing down. He had no face to go back. Ananya had shut the door on his face.

He wished he had just one chance to tell her, "I love you Ananya, I can't live without you. Come back, please come back, please."

Chapter 12

Priya
Guwahati
February 1997

"Samarth I am leaving for the day. Please don't forget to e-mail that information to the head office. They're waiting."

The boss hurried out shouting out the instructions.

Samarth hated it particularly when he was himself preparing to wrap up for the day. But nothing doing, it was the boss's order after all.

With a frown Samarth sat before the computer again. Tired fingers worked on the key board as he started mailing some necessary bit of information to the head office in kolkata.

"Bijuuuu", he shouted for the office peon, "get me a cup of black tea".

There was no other way to fight away the sleep that threatened to heavily settle on his eyes. It had been a long day for him too.

Looking at the amount of matter that still needed to be typed, Samarth decided to let it go for the time being, at least till the tea came.

"Meantime let me check my own mails."

He navigated to the mail box. It was almost a month now that Ananya's mails had stopped coming. She wrote beautiful poems which he loved reading. But it was all over now. The fantastic dream was over and illusions had succumbed to the onslaught of reality.

"No I will not think of her", Samarth said to himself with gritted jaws. He had struggled hard and alone all through the last month to cope with the pain.

Ever since Ananya left he had stopped talking about emotions. He did not even let JC know about the turmoil and agony that he went through everyday.

He was gradually learning to accept it all and get over it so he wouldn't allow himself to grow weak again.

"What's this?" browsing through innumerable unread mails, his cursor suddenly stood still on one name.

"*Priya*? After so many years?"

It was a short mail like always. She never wrote long ones. It read as follows,

Hi sam, I am back. Tried hard to forget everything but couldn't.

How's life been for you? I am sure it was boring without me. Chicago was beautiful but not more exciting than you. I missed our fights and your passionate kisses. Will wait for you in the same old place at 5.30 on valentine's day. You remember na?of course you do. Can Sam ever forget her Priya? Love you. Will wait for you.

Priya

Samarth looked at the mail for a long time. He read and re read it, unable to believe himself. The mail had been waiting in his box, unchecked for over a fortnight.

"But how can this be possible? Priya is back from abroad and she says she's back for me?"

Three years back Priya Sharma had literally ditched him for a career abroad and had not even thought twice about the man she was leaving behind, broken and shattered.

Samarth leaned back in his chair and tried to recollect some fading memories.

It was way back in the year 1992. He had gone to the Premium Club to attend a Journalists' party. There he met Rajni Behl, his ex—colleague from The North-East Times.

Rajni was accompanied by her cousin Priya.

"Hey Sam, meet her. She is my cousin Priya.

Priya Sharma."

"Hi", Samarth could barely speak. He was already bowled over by the tall, slim, extremely attractive lady standing in front of her. She had brown eyes, a sharp nose above a pair of thin delicate lips. Her fair complexion was only accentuated by her straight, long shiny black hair. The youthful curves of her body were teasing from beneath her body hugging sea green top and a wrap—around of a darker shade. She was full and firm, youthfulness haughtily exuded by every single feature of hers

Is she real or a dream?" Samarth wondered as did almost every young man present there.

"If there is anything called love at first sight, I am in love with her", he said to himself.

"Care for a drink?" Samarth offered when Rajni went to the other part of the hall to meet some old friends, trusting her cousin to his care.

"A fresh lime juice if possible".

"Yeah sure." Samarth almost dashed to the soft drink counter.

It was a pleasure watching the pretty lass accepting the glass from him thankfully.

"She's breathtaking!" Samarth thought.

"What do you do Priya?" He asked.

I just completed my MBA from Symbiosis Pune and currently I am doing some research work on behalf of the Enviornmental department of the Maharashtra government, in collaboration with the IIT Guwahati."

"That's impressive. Let me know if I can be of any help, it would be a privilege to be associated with you".

Priya laughed and Samarth felt there were only rainbows all around him. His entire world had merged with this one figure, the beautiful woman standing in front of him.

"Care for a dance Samarth?"

Samarth felt butterflies fluttering in his stomach and wondered if he had heard her correct.

As if realizing his confusion, Priya repeated, "how about a dance Samarth?"

"Sure" Samarth almost stammered before guiding an amused Priya on to the floor.

As he touched her waist lightly, he felt a shiver down his spine.

Priya was lithe and graceful in his fold and Samarth was acutely conscious of her closeness. The warmth of her breath, the tantalizing fragrance of her body, her soft hand in his was driving him crazy.

He could sense several pairs of jealous eyes piercing him as they floated across the floor to the rhythm of music. He prayed for time to stop and the moment to linger for ever and for ever.

"Sir . . . . Tea", the peon's voice jerked him back from his reverie.

Samarth took a careful sip from the steaming cup and went back to his world of reverie.

Since that evening the affair between Samarth Bose and Priya Sharma had been the talk of the town.

The duo stole the show anywhere they went. They were smart, adventurous, vivacious and looked really good together. Samarth loved to flaunt Priya before his friends. They all envied his luck except JC.

For some reason he was very reserved with his comments on Priya.

Through the first one year of their affair Samarth felt he was in the seventh heaven. He would literally run out of the office at the end of the day to be with Priya. He thought this kind of love only existed in the fairy tales but never had he imagined that it could be possible in reality.

Priya was pretty, smart, intelligent, daring and ambitious. The only problem she had, was a nasty temper but that was always short—lived.

"But then who on earth is perfect? We all have our share of defects", Samir would argue with himself.

Trouble started around the middle of 1993.

Priya seemed to be getting more and more involved in her career activities, so much so that they hardly had time to meet.

Of course Samarth never had any objection to that. On the contrary he had always been supportive about her career. She was such a bright scholar and she deserved to make it big in life someday.

It was November 19th, Priya's birthday.

Samarth had been busy for over a week unable to decide what gift to choose for his princess. She had decided to spend a quiet birthday this year, in the exclusive company of Samarth. Needless to say Samarth wanted to make it very very special.

"But how do I make the day special for her? What is it that would touch her heart?" Samarth kept thinking.

Finally on the eve of her birthday he was able to decide on something and he was sure that his surprise would touch her soul.

The dinner was at *Capri*, one of the best and most expensive food joints in the city. It was a roof-top restaurant and had live bands performing everyday.

The couple was dressed perfectly for the occasion.

Priya looked breathtaking in her pink *mekhla* embroidered with sky blue thread with shell—pink pearl accessories to match. She smelt sweet and wore her characteristic half-smile that sent so many hearts fluttering. Samarth sported a rust coloured Lee T-shirt over a pair of off—white khakis and smelt strongly of *old spice* after-shave lotion that Priya loved so much.

"Happy Birthday darling", Samarth had said, lightly kissing her cheek, in the elevator, on their way up to the eighth floor terrace where Samarth had kept their tables reserved.

On reaching the restaurant Samarth whispered something into the ears of the nearest waiter who smiled and nodded. The next moment they were being guided to their seats and Priya beamed on setting her eyes on the table. There on the center of the table stood a double-storeyed chocolate cake with a lemon coloured strawberry topping. In the center of it was written

To you, for whom my heart beats

and inside the alphabet 'a' of the word 'heart' was fixed a rose-shaped candle, waiting to be lit. A knife with a satin red ribbon tied to it was lying in a tray on the table, beside the cake.

Priya was visibly overwhelmed. Samarth's heart melted at the sight of those eyes that held his own, with tender love and exuberant joy.

"This is all I wanted God, just to see her happy, very very happy" Samarth thought.

Then as he silently motioned to Priya to pick up the knife and cut the cake, she obeyed shyly. She moved towards the table to first blow out the candle that Samarth had already lit for her. Just as she puffed it out, the band played the happy birthday chime and the few people present there clapped, sending her off to uncontrollable giggles like a school girl.

Samarth watched her and felt, "I can do anything in the world just to see her smiling like this"

Having fed the first slice of cake to each other they passed the remaining pieces to the waiters around who accepted it gratefully. After all not every patron visiting their eatery everyday was so generous.

"Sir you have a call on the second line", Biju's voice hurled Samarth back to the present.

"Ok, I am coming".

It was boss.

"This man cannot trust anybody with any work", Samarth was irritated.

He had assured him he would send the mails to the head office but the boss wouldn't feel sure without giving at least five reminders personally.

Thankfully the conversation was brief.

Samarth returned to his table and quickly finished the job. There were three mails to be sent, one long and two short. He was in a hurry to reach home too. Wrapping up his own work quickly, Samarth had a last look at the disorienting mail, shut the computer down and sped towards the car that had been waiting for the last one hour to drop him home.

Samarth also wanted to release the driver quickly. He was an old man and looked very tired at such late hours of the day.

No sooner did he hop into the car, than the engine roared and they were racing down the quiet, dark roads of the sleeping city, towards Samarth's residence at Navinnagar.

With nothing else in the outside world to distract or disrupt his attention, Samarth's thoughts drifted back to the roof-top at *Capri*.

The birthday dinner had begun with white wine as they drank to each other's well-being and love.

It was followed by a sumptuous dinner of mouth-watering moghlai dishes, Priya's favourite.

As they were waiting for the waiter to get the bill, Priya touched Samarth's hand softly.

"Thanks Sam, for such a wonderful birthday gift".

Reading the question in his eyes, she added, "I mean such a special party".

"But you are yet to get your birthday gift sweetheart", Samarth chirped.

He enjoyed the astonishment on her face.

"You mean my day isn't over yet?" Priya asked trying to suppress her excitement.

"No my Princess, how can it be without your birthday gift?"

So saying he drew from his trouser pocket a small blue velvet box and held it open in front of her startled eyes.

"I love you Priya. Will you marry me?"

Samarth's voice quivered with emotion.

The sparkling white diamond set in a simple yet exquisite gold band seemed to reflect the spirit of the man standing in front of him.

But Priya's heart sank. She didn't know how to react. It had all happened so suddenly and so unexpectedly. Samarth hadn't given her any hint about it, otherwise she could have explained.

But she had to say something now.

He was looking at her expectantly with the ring in his hand.

"I am sorry Sam, I am terribly sorry but I am not ready for it yet", was all she could whisper.

As if unable to believe what he had just heard, Samarth pleaded, "Priya please don't say like that. I know, I know it has happened all too suddenly . . . . my fault you see, but you can always take your time . . . we can always settle sometime next year but please don't say *no* priya please don't say . . . ." his voice had choked.

"Can we talk about it later Sam? I want to go home."

They drove home quietly, not having anything to say. As he watched her disappear behind the tall iron gates of her house that night, Samarth suddenly felt his life was going away from him and he didn't know what to do. An excruciating, inexplicable pain seemed to stab at his heart and he wanted to yell like a helpless, dumb animal.

"Sir, you are home", Old Monk's voice interrupted his thoughts again.

Samarth walked past the main gate of the compound. Before reaching for the stairs leading to his flat in the first floor, he exchanged the customary greetings with the Nightwatchman. He was the only one to greet him every night when he returned. Rest of the complex normally remained asleep at this time, including his mother and sister.

Reaching his flat Samarth took out the keys and unlocked the door. Though mom always insisted on opening the door herself, Samarth didn't let her. Doctor had strictly advised her against staying up late.

Even Ishita had morning school, so he didn't expect her to wait either.

Freshening up quickly, he moved to the kitchen.

His dinner was kept ready inside the microwave oven.

Samarth put the switch on and waited for a couple of minutes to warm the food. He then proceeded with the plate of *roti*, *sabji* and egg curry and a bottle of water, to the drawing room.

Planting himself comfortably on the sofa, he reached for the remote, switched on the TV and minimized the volume, careful not to wake up anybody.

For the next ten minutes that he needed to finish his food, Samarth tried to concentrate on a wild life programme coming on the channel Animal Planet.

The day had been long and tiring and he could hardly wait to hit the bed.

But sleep eluded him that night.

Samarth looked at the phone lying quietly beside his pillow.

Suddenly he felt desperate. He wanted the phone to buzz. He wanted to hear it ring, the very ring that he normally cursed throughout the day.

He remembered how he had waited for the phone to ring on that night of 19th November, four years ago.

"What is happening to me?" Samarth wondered.

Memories of the bygone years were flooding back but someone else was in his mind.

It was not long before Samarth realized he was missing *Ananya*. He felt an irresistible desire to talk to her.

Instead, at half past two in the night, Samarth Bose found himself dialing some other number, trying to reach somebody who he knew would be comforting to talk to . . . . most importantly who alone would entertain his call at such weird hour.

"Yes Samarth, what's up?" JC's voice came floating from the other side.

Chapter 13

The phone call
Guwahati
20 Nov, 1993.
1.15am

The phone call had come, but on the following night. By that time Samarth had been through a thousand hells, spent a sleepless, peace less night and even missed office.

Priya hadn't called or messaged even once throughout the day.

"Doesn't she understand what I am going through?" Samarth had wondered. He tried calling on Priya's mobile phone several times but it had been switched off since the previous night.

"Why doesn't she talk to me once? Is the issue so complicated that it can't be talked out?" Samarth could not help wondering. But a silenced phone frustrated all his efforts to communicate, again and again.

When finally his cell phone rang at quarter past one in the night, flashing Priya's number, Samarth felt too numb to react.

"Hello", his voice was muffled.

"Hello Sam", Priya said in a controlled voice.

A long silence followed.

"What went wrong honey? I am sorry if I was being too persuasive", Samarth tried to come straight to the point.

"We can always wait", he added hurriedly in an attempt to control any damage that might have been done.

"It's not a question of waiting Sam, that's what I need to clarify to you".

"Then what is the problem? Everything was perfect till yesterday evening. And I told you I am sorry about the proposal." Samarth sounded desperate.

"I can't marry you Sam. Not now, not ever. My scholarship has been granted by the University of Chicago and I am leaving next month."

"But Priya . . . ."

"Please try to understand Sam", Priya interrupted.

"It's been my dream to go abroad for higher studies and settle there. I can't sacrifice my dream for stupid emotional considerations . . . ."

"Come again", this time Priya was stopped in the middle of her outburst.

"Please come again Priya, did I hear you correct?

"Stupid emotional considerations . . . . is that what you said?"

Priya could discern the shock and disbelief in Samarth's voice. But there was little she could do about it. Of course she was fond of Samarth, he was a sweet guy but not so important for whom she could sacrifice her career.

In fact why Samarth, no body in her life was worth so much. And hadn't she turned down lucrative proposals already from far more eligible, prospective grooms than Samarth Bose?

Who was Samarth Bose after all?

An ordinary journalist from an ordinary middle class family without ambition, without dreams, without any hunger for success or recognition. Yes he was fun for company but how could he think so bold . . . . marriage and all that! My foot!

"Priya I asked you something . . . damn it answer me",. Samarth's demanding tone flared up her temper.

"Yes of course you heard me correct. I can't put up with too much of that *love* stuff *Yaar*.

Dates were okay but life—long commitment? God! I am sorry, I can't even think about it."

"Enough Priya!" Samarth found himself yelling.

Priya's outburst had been a bolt out of the blue. Torment and agony gave way to anger and humiliation.

He felt like a fool, his pride injured, his dignity undermined.

"You think I was dating you over the last one year simply for fun? Tell me you never understood my feelings were serious! Didn't I tell you I was planning to talk to mom about us? Answer me Priya, I demand a god damned answer"

Samarth was shouting now, unaware that his mother and sister had woken up hearing him yell and were lying in their bed in the next room, tensed and anxious.

"How dare you demand an explanation? Even my parents don't talk to me in that tone Samarth." Priya snapped back bitterly.

"Yeah I know, but I wish they had, so that you would have learnt to respect feelings and behave human" He was caustic beyond control now.

"Shut up Samarth. Don't you dare cross your limits? You dare to criticize my parents? Look at yours . . . a bunch of bloody middle class dreamers . . . . Yes that's what you people are, sentimental fools . . . . A whole lot of hypocrites using outcries of morals and values to cover up for failures. I hate you and the whole lot of you", Priya was spewing venom now.

Samarth thought he had never before seen Priya so nakedly exposed with all her crudities.

Without a word more he slammed the phone down.

He didn't realize how long since then he had remained sitting with his head held in his hand. His face was moist with tears of anger and humiliation and his head throbbed, probably still reeling under the impact of disillusionment.

When he got up from his place, the eastern sky was already flushed with the pink hue of the rising sun. The birds had started twittering and few morning walkers could be heard downstairs waiting for the others to join them for their regular stroll in the nearby park.

Chapter 14

The Valentine's Day
Guwahati
February14, 1997

The night before had passed without sleep.

"Should I go or shouldn't I?Was she serious or was it another of her cruel whimsical jokes?"

The dilemma had tormented Samarth throughout the night. It was impossible for him to ignore or forget Priya's mail. More than any hope, it was curiosity that was making him uncontrollably restless.

"What does Priya Sharma want after so many days?"

Samarth kept guessing wildly.

The clock seemed to have got stuck on that day for Samarth and 5.30 seemed long long away. He had been sitting ready since 3 in the afternoon. He had already informed office about his early leave that day, only time seemed to have stopped moving.

"Old place should mean her small studio—apartment at Stadium Road", Samarth tried to remember.

"That's where we had celebrated the two intimate Valentine's Day together", a sudden surge of memories made him twitch uneasily.

"Hope I am not making a mistake taking her seriously again", an empty feeling inside the stomach made Samarth feel slightly ill at ease as he crawled inside the taxi.

"Stadium Road *bhaia*", Samarth could feel the rising tension in his own voice.

He was tensed because he was not in control of the situation. He felt as if he was in some kind of trance, not exactly aware of what was going on but acting nevertheless.

When the taxi pulled up in front of the Gitanjali Apartment, it was 5.26 by his watch.

Four years back this used to be a frequent haunt for him. So many lazy, languid evenings he had spent here with Priya. But today the same old building looked so strange and imposing.

"I hope this is where she meant by the same old place in her mail", suddenly Samarth felt drained of all confidence.

With slow, hesitant steps he entered the building and turned towards the staircase. He deliberately chose not to use the elevator, trying to give himself some time before this awkward meeting.

As he started climbing towards Priya's third floor apartment, Samarth tried to relax. Thankfully the old caretaker of the apartment was not in his seat when Samarth entered the building. The man knew him and about his relationship with Priya pretty well. It would have been awkward to face him after two long years.

Samarth was taken by surprise to find the door of the flat left slightly ajar. He didn't need to ring the doorbell.

"Am I expected for sure or is it a mistake?" He wondered.

Still he knocked twice on the door. There was no response.

"Priya?" Samarth called out.

He was uttering this name after a very long time and he felt that his voice had gone dry.

Samarth pushed open the door and stepped in.

The drawing room had the same old familiar décor of two big leather couches with a glass-top center table placed on a thick Persian carpet and a beautiful painting of galloping horses hanging over the pure mahogany dining table that occupied the south-east corner of the room.

What arrested Samarth's attention was the bunch of fresh smelling red roses arranged carefully in an exquisite bone-china vase on the center table. Right beside it was a tempting looking chocolate cake with Happy Valentine's Day written on it. And resting lightly against the edge of the plate containing the cake, sat a small, cute, white teddy holding a red heart in his hands on which it was written *always yours.*

Samarth could feel his heartbeat rising. Life seemed to have taken a u-turn and the flow of Time had reversed.

This was exactly how Priya had greeted him on the Valentine's Day during those two years. Nothing had changed. She hadn't forgotten anything.

Priya Sharma, his lost love, was back in his life.

"Hello Sam".

The familiar, intoxicating husky voice made Samarth look up. He felt his blood charged as he found himself facing the same old Priya, gorgeous and breathtaking.

She was donned in an exquisite, blood-red, soft chiffon sari that clung to her body and her straight long hair was done up in a top-knot held lightly by a delicate pin.

Her matching red blouse was held in place by only two thin laces for straps, knotted up at the shoulder on both sides and the neckline plunged deep enough to boldly reveal the cleavage between the full curves.

Besides a pair of red ear studs, she wasn't wearing any accessory. Her long slender arms were bare and so was her neck. Through the transparent layer of the chiffon, her deep naval, sporting a ring that held the skin in a fold, exhibited itself tantalizingly.

Her eyes seemed unreal under the effect of the deep liner and heavy shade. The glossy red lipstick made her lips more desirable than they already were.

"*She is dressed to kill*", Samarth thought. But he had to admit that Priya was still irresistible.

She commanded the same ravishing figure with full and deep curves accentuating it at the right places.

"Hello", Samarth smiled back.

"I knew you would come", she was moving towards him.

Samarth tried to make his way towards the couch before Priya wriggled past him towards the door and locked it.

"So how's life dear", Samarth tried to breathe and act normal.

"Oh fantastic" Priya replied in her familiar enthusiastic tone "except for one thing I was missing and that's why I am back".

"And what's that?" The question blurted out of his mouth before Samarth could control it.

"Ah ha you still haven't guessed the reason Sam?" she bent teasingly over him, before planting herself on the couch, beside him, flashing her captivating smile all through.

As the bare skin of her soft arms brushed against his, Samarth felt his resistance dropping. He stiffened in an attempt to gain control.

"Care for some wine Sam? The same old white stuff, your favourite . . . ?" she whispered in his ear.

Samarth nodded. More than the wine it was necessary to free himself from the dangerous proximity of this irresistible woman.

He had decided to be very careful today. He would guard himself consciously against getting carried away.

Before going to fetch the wine, Priya had tuned in a soft instrumental piece and the music filled every corner of the room. The mellow light filtering through the two Japanese shades in the two corners of the room lent it a dreamy touch.

Priya was back with the wine. She carefully placed them on the dining table. Then she moved towards the center table again and knelt down on the carpet.

"Let's first celebrate Sam, it's Valentine's Day?" She beckoned him to come near the table.

Samarth obeyed quietly.

Priya put the ribboned knife in his hand and then took his hand in her own. As the knife ripped through the soft chocolate, Priya whispered sensuously, *"Happy Valentine's Day, my love . . . ."*

"Same to you Priya, thanks a lot for this beautiful evening once again" Samarth replied.

"This is for you and it carries my exclusive message for you on this special day", Priya said, holding up the teddy for Samarth.

"But I forgot to get any gift for you Priya", he said, suddenly embarrassed.

"No darling, you had already given me the gift of a lifetime, I was too immature to realize its worth then", Priya sighed.

"Does she regret?" Samarth wondered. He was not too sure.

Priya now sliced off a solid chunk of the cake and held it for Samarth to take a bite.

He bit into it and offered to do the same.

Priya took his hand and started licking the cream off his fingers.

The touch of her warm moist tongue made Samarth feel weak all over. He fought himself quietly.

Priya had gone back to the dining table to fetch the wine glasses.

As the glasses clinked against each other to cheer the occasion, Priya muttered, "To the reunion of parted lovers" and laughed.

She had now snuggled up to Samarth in the broad comfortable couch.

For the next few minutes they sipped their drinks in silence. The dizzy effect of the drink had begun to take over which they both enjoyed.

Suddenly Samarth felt a strange void inside him.

Why wasn't he feeling that maddening excitement, why wasn't he exactly enjoying? What more could he have wanted? His lost love was back to him, they were celebrating their reunion on none other than the Valentine's Day and dark days were over.

"What else do I need to feel high and happy?" Samarth rebuked himself.

But a shocking, momentary feeling chilled him for a while. He felt he was missing *Ananya*.

"Oh no!" samarth pushed aside the thought. He simply couldn't afford to spoil this evening at any cost. It was too special to be wasted away like this. He forced his mind back on Priya.

She was now looking up at him with her red lips parted slightly. A drop of the wine still rested on her lower lip. Samarth bent his mouth and lightly licked it off her lip. Then as he attempted to straighten himself, Priya pulled his face down on hers.

"Kiss me Sam, the way you always did", her voice was hoarse and she was breathing fast. Her teeth dug softly into the lobe of Samarth's left ear.

He started licking the lipstick off her lips, softly rolling his tongue over them. Soon they were kissing each other furiously, passionately, every passing moment witnessing their hunger for each other.

Priya was now half reclining beneath him. With the *pallu* of her sari already off her shoulders, she was provocatively close.

Samarth undid the shoulder laces with perfect ease.

He touched her bare skin and felt himself growing hard against her. He kissed her vigorously again, all over from the neck to the cleavage and traveled down towards the naval. Her soft moans excited him. He pulled her naval ring out with his teeth and spat it on the floor. His tongue teased her naval.

Samarth was electrified. *"I can't wait any longer honey"*, he whispered.

Flames of passion were ablaze. Priya's cries of pleasure made him plunge deeper and deeper inside her. And now the passions were bursting, exploding. Samarth held her closer and tighter. Her long nails dug deep on his back, her teeth bit into his arms to hold back the cries, and soon there was a blissful release.

He was trembling in ecstasy as he kept muttering, *"I love you, I love you, I love you **Ananya**"*.

But his voice was drowned in the loud moan that Priya emitted during the final moment of rapture.

They lay in each other's arms quietly for some time.

The spell was broken when Priya kissed his forehead and said, "Let me order for dinner Sam, a nice little Chinese joint has come up just round the corner, their ginger chicken is fantastic".

Samarth sat up, picked up his clothes and moved towards the washroom. "No *yaar*, it's already late. *Ma* will be waiting over dinner." Samarth said.

"But you can always call up and inform her . . . . we are meeting after such a long time Sam", she sounded hurt.

"No Priya, you know it well, I don't skip dinner at home without prior intimation. You see old habits die hard", he laughed over his shoulder before closing the door of the washroom.

"The same old crap", Priya said to herself. Disgust had already replaced all the pleasures of the evening.

But she chose to maintain silence.

On his way back home that evening, Samarth felt strangely disturbed. He was still reeling under the impact of the evening but there was one thought that dominated his mind above everything and he failed to fight it off.

He was thinking of *Ananya* and only *Ananya*. But he couldn't understand why.

Chapter 15

Another Valentine
Madhabpur
West Bengal
February 14, 1997

"Sister Kuhelika, there's a call for you from Kolkata. It's urgent, *guruji* said. The call is on hold, please come fast," the urgency oozed from fourteen year old Subal's voice. He had come running on his errand and was panting for breath.

The ashram compound was pretty big and from the office room in the main building to the garden in the backyard was quite a distance. Of course Subal knew that from 5 to 5.30 in the evening Sister Kuhelika was to be found in the backyard flower garden, watering the plants. It was her daily routine and every ashramite like Subal knew it. They had known it since their childhood. So he didn't have to waste time looking for her.

"Any problem at home?" Sister Kuhelika wondered. Years of meditation had cured her of any kind of tension but she couldn't help feeling concerned still. She just hoped that her father was fine. He had never quite recovered from the major stroke that he suffered fifteen years back when she had announced her decision to become an ashramite under the guidance of his *gurudev*.

Since that time he had always some or the other complaints related to health. Even the pacemaker failed to stabilize his heart anymore.

She moved towards the main building with brisk steps.

Guruji was seated at the desk when she entered the office room. Sensing her anxiety beneath the calm exterior, he motioned towards the phone and said, "Some lady from Kolkata . . . . insisted on talking to you . . . . said it's very urgent."

Anxiety gave way to surprise. It's been a long time since personal calls had stopped coming. Hardly anybody had this number unless a close acquaintance of the family.

She looked at *guruji* once before picking up the receiver. He was busy replying the letters of the patrons.

"Hello, Sister Kuhelika here"

"Hello Kuhu"

Sister Kuhelika felt a shudder. In the last one decade, since she had become a complete *sanyasini* no body called her by this name . . . not even her parents. If anything ever disturbed her, it was any reference to her past. She had renounced her old life by choice, by a mere urge to dedicate herself to the service of humanity, and not by any compulsion.

The day she had made up her mind to give up that life, she had given up everything . . . . her pleasures, ambitions, relations and even the name.

Guruji had been her spiritual guide all through and it was he who had re-christened her as sister kuhelika the day she came to the ashram years back, at the age of eighteen.

"Kuhu this is Ananya . . . . I am in trouble kuhu; I need your help . . . . there's no one else I can turn to".

Ananya.

The name made her mind race back to her school, Saint Mariana Convent in Durgapur. Almost in an instant a few faces overlapped, laughing, chirping, fighting, flashed before her eyes in a misty vision.

"What happened Kuhu? Don't you remember me? I am *Ananya*, your . . . ."

Sister Kuhelika interrupted the desperate voice.

She said calmly, "I am Sister Kuhelika but I remember you. People come to us in trouble. Tell me your problem ".

The next ten minutes the young *sanyasini* listened silently and intently. Before replacing the phone she only said, "let me talk to *guruji* and I shall let you know what to do by tomorrow morning. Have faith in God. All will be well."

Guruji had not looked up even once during her conversation. At the end of it he only asked, "Is everything well Kuhelika?"

"I need to talk to you *guruji*, someone needs our help", Sister Kuhelika said. "Can I talk to you sometime later tonight after your evening puja?" she asked.

"You can talk to me now if you wish. I have almost finished replying the letters."

For the next half an hour Sister Kuhelika was engaged in a long and serious discussion with *guruji*

His decision at the end of it all filled her with immense joy. But apparently she maintained her calm.

Before leaving the room she thanked *guruji* wholeheartedly.

Far away in her *Behala* apartment in Kolkata, Ananya was busy preparing herself to take yet another plunge in life, and this time probably the toughest one.

Ever since she had returned from the Dr.Ghosh's clinic, her mind had not been at rest. She felt confused under the mixed impact of joy, excitement and nervousness.

Two days back she had visited the doctor complaining of some indigestion problem. But it had not even occurred remotely to Ananya that it could be a serious issue.

Having finished his preliminary examination, Dr.Ghosh had very hesitantly suggested that Ananya should take a pregnancy test. She was too shocked to refuse.

This morning he had called up Ananya personally to inform that she had tested positive and must visit him immediately.

"You are in the very first month of your pregnancy Ananya and during the next two months you got to be very very careful with yourself," the aged doctor had said sagaciously.

"The baby should be due sometime in the first week of October, if everything goes right" he had explained. "Till that time you must come for regular check-ups every month. If possible have somebody to escort you when you come."

His final words made her soul bleed.

How would Ananya explain to the doctor that no one was going to escort her, no one was going to stand by her . . . . there would be no joy or celebration for her motherhood. It was her lone crusade and she would have to fight it out alone.

Chapter 16

The Lone Battle
Kolkata/madhabpur
February–September
1997

The sky in the afternoon of June 20th was murky. The rain seemed to be holding out like the welled up tears in their eyes. None of them spoke a word.

Siddharth, the more emotional of the two broke the silence.

"When will you come back *mom*?" His voice faltered.

"I don't know really", Ananya replied honestly.

"Can't we come down to meet you sometime?" This time it was Vivek. The desperation in the voice which he fought to suppress, didn't escape Ananya's ears.

"There isn't even mobile network there you said. Then how do we keep in touch *mom*?"

"And what do we tell the others when they ask about you? Even if we pretend ignorance, they'll never believe us", Siddharth said helplessly.

"I'll keep calling the two of you from time to time", Ananya tried to console them. "To the others you can always say that I am out of town for a few months to complete some writing assignment"

"Once I come back, I'll explain everything to everyone", Ananya promised.

It was 3.16 by the watch. The Howrah-Madhabpur local was scheduled to depart from the Howrah station at 3.20. Fortunately the train was not too crowded and Ananya had come with enough time in hand to manage a comfortable seat by the window.

A small suitcase, her only luggage was placed under the seat as in these trains there was no luggage bunk on top. Daily passengers only commuted by these trains to go and return from their workplaces in the city. So hardly did anybody need to carry any luggage.

The final whistle pierced her ears. The iron wheels had begun to roll on the metal tracks. Ananya stretched out her hands to hold the hands of her boys.

The train was crawling along the platform. Siddharth and Vivek started walking briskly to keep pace with the window that was moving away. Some last minute passengers were busy running along side the moving train to board it.

The two boys were now running on the platform, their hands still held in hers but threatening to slip away any moment. Ananya felt her control was giving away. Tears now streamed down her eyes like a torrential downpour. Outside on the platform the two boys were crying uncontrollably as they ran, least bothered about the several pairs of eyes looking at them curiously.

The train was gathering speed now, it had almost covered the length of the platform.

"We'll miss you *mom*, please take care", Vivek shouted as he felt her fingers slipping away from his own.

The hold broken, the two boys were now running hard, gasping for breath. Ananya couldn't even motion them to stop. She was barely in control of herself.

"We'll wait for you *mom*. Please come back soon", Siddharth shouted to make himself heard over the deep rumbling sound of the rolling metals and the general clamour of the people, hawkers and other trains departing and arriving.

Ananya pressed her cheeks hard against the iron bars of the window and strained her eyes to catch a last glimpse of her children who were standing on the edge of the platform waving at her. They were now receding fast from her vision and with them the city, her family, her relationships and everything that she had ever called her own.

Wiping her tears, ananya tried to relax on her seat. There were five more passengers, two men and three women in the far-end of her seat. The two men were dozing. Two women were busy talking to each other and the third, an old woman with a rustic appearance looked at Ananya intently. In fact she had been watching her since the time she was talking to her boys.

Ananya felt irritatingly conscious. She looked out of the window. The sky was overcast now and the grey was steadily deepening to a black. A light drizzle had already started but the cool breeze felt soothing in the otherwise sultry June afternoon.

Half closing the shutter of the window, Ananya closed her eyes. The goings had been very tough for her over the last four months and only God knew what lay ahead.

It had been a bold decision not to go for an abortion.

"How can I kill them? They are our children. Mine and Samarth's . . . ." she had told herself again and again. So what if she didn't want to bother Samarth with any unwelcome responsibility, she could still manage on her own.

"God I need a miracle, send me an angel to show me the right path. Save this mother from doing any sin, please God", she had prayed that day with the faith and devotion that she had once learnt in school from Sister Mariana.

And her prayer had been answered. God had sent her the angel to protect her and her children.

Kuhu was nothing less than an angel in her life. It was she, who after listening to her entire story had spoken to *guruji* and arranged for her shelter in the ashram.

Her children would be born there, away from the scathing, critical, questioning, accusing society.

Few people knew about her pregnancy.

Her parents had been shocked and broken. Her father had stopped talking to her ever since and she had only a brief conversation with her mother.

"Sayan had half-killed your father, now you finished the rest. Please never come to this house again, the condition of his heart is not good and I don't want to give him any stress."

Ma had spoken the words in a single breath the last time she had spoken to her and replaced the phone. She had not even wanted to know about the father of her children.

Before sharing everything with Vivek and Siddharth, Ananya had thought thousand times over.

They were both matured and sensitive but Ananya was scared about their reaction to her decision of going away.

It indeed had been tough and took her long to make them understand the practical side of things and bring them into her way of thinking.

None of the boys however needed to be told that the secret they had been entrusted with should go with them to their graves unless their *mom* chose to reveal it herself.

Her last but certainly not the least confidant was JC. She couldn't keep such a big issue from her *bro*, her only link with Samarth. She had mailed him all details including her future plans regarding herself and her children and he had offered to come down immediately to fetch her.

"You come and stay with me in Guwahati, *sis*. Samarth won't know anything, I promise", he had pleaded over the phone.

His concern had overwhelmed Ananya but she insisted on sticking to her own plans, of course promising to keep in touch always.

He in turn had promised faithfully never to let Samarth know anything about her.

The last thing that Ananya could put up in life with was the pity of the man whom she loved and who did not love her.

The next four months had passed with lightening speed.

Ananya knew she couldn't conceal her pregnancy till after another four months at best. She had to wrap up her pending work, complete teaching the syllabus to her students within their summer vacation which was to last from May 20th to June 20th.

Everyday she worked double shifts to cope with the pressure to the best of her ability, careful at the same time not to over-exert in her condition.

Dr. Ghosh had been more than just a doctor during this period. He treated her almost with paternal affection and Ananya felt grateful. Even at the weird hours of night, whenever she felt the slightest discomfort, he came running to comfort this girl who was about his daughter's age.

He never told Ananya about her only daughter who had died at childbirth in the process of delivering her second issue.

Ananya's friends, colleagues, relatives and students were all told that Ananya was going out of town for a few months to do some writing assignment on behalf of a publication company. No further clarification was needed because she wasn't that close to anyone except her children.

But at night she would wet her pillow with tears. She felt like running into her mother's arms the way she did during her childhood days or bury her face in her father's chest and stay quietly in his embrace.

"I need you *ma*, I need you *baba* . . . . why don't you listen to me?" she would yell at times at the dark ceiling.

The train suddenly screeched to a halt. It was dark outside now. A light drizzle was still on.

They had not halted at any station. Some hawker must have pulled the emergency chain to get down at his comfortable point, an usual practice with the hawkers.

Ananya noticed that the compartment was almost full now but everybody had a seat.

It was 5.10 by her watch. She bought a cup of coffee from a hawker and asked, "*dada* how long will it take to reach Madhabpur?"

"The train is running about 20 minutes late *didi* but you should reach by 7", he replied while pouring the coffee.

"Still a long way!" Ananya sighed.

That evening when Ananya got off the train at Madhabpur station, it was well past 7.30.

She stepped carefully on the dark platform along with two other passengers. She could hear the rain beating heavily on the station shed and blinked to get herself adjusted to the darkness around.

"Are you *Ananya didi* from kolkata?"

Startled to hear her name, Ananya turned round and found herself looking into the eyes of a village boy in his middle teens. He was holding up an oil lamp in which Ananya saw his face.

"Yes", she nodded.

"I am Subal, I stay in the ashram. *Guruji* and Sister Kuhelika have sent me to fetch you. They have sent car." He introduced himself while taking the suitcase from Ananya.

"Ok", Ananya smiled. She felt relieved that Kuhu had sent someone to receive her.

When she crawled inside an old, rather shabby looking Ambassador, she heard Subal explaining, "this car jumps a lot *didi*. It was donated to the ashram for office work only. The roads are not good and it is raining. You please sit carefully".

As the car bumped along the dark, wet, uneven, muddy roads of Madhabpur, with an old driver at the wheels, Subal kept on talking.

Not that Ananya was listening to all of it very carefully but she enjoyed the company of this simple, innocent village lad.

Chapter 17

Reunion with Angels
Karunashram
Madhabpur

"Had a nice sleep?"
Ananya found Kuhu smiling down at her.

The smile wasn't exactly the enthusiastic or excited smile of a friend meeting another old friend, after years . . . . but assuring and comforting nevertheless.

Kuhu had never been very expressive, Ananya remembered.

"*Sister Kuhelika*", she corrected herself silently.

"Yes", she replied, smiling back.

During the few hours of last night Ananya had got habituated to see her dressed in a milk white *sari* with a high-neck, full sleeve blouse and the hair done up neatly in a knot.

"She is an embodiment of perfect peace", Ananya reflected.

"I have a nice little surprise for you today", Sister Kuhelika said as Ananya sat up on her bed.

"You get ready, have your bath and breakfast, and someone will come to fetch you in another hour or so. Meanwhile I'll finish my *puja* and meditation."

"And yes send for Subal, if you need anything. He is weeding the garden outside", Sister Kuhelika said as she left the room.

Ananya stretched herself on the bed.

After almost four months she had slept so well.

Waking up to the chirping of birds instead of honking horns of vehicles plying on the city roads was also a welcome and novel experience.

As she left the bed and stood up, the mud floor felt cool beneath her feet. Though every corner of the mud-walled, thatch-roofed room was basking in the morning sun, it was still quite cool inside in these early hours of morning.

She had been given one of the ten guest-huts that the ashram maintained to accommodate distant visitors or patrons.

Each of these huts had a rope cot for a bed with a thick straw cover for a mattress. It was softer and more comfortable then anything she had ever laid on.

For Ananya, Sister kuhelika had arranged for a special wooden cupboard and a writing desk and a chair occupying two corners of the room. A mirror hung on one side of the wall.

Ananya was not a visitor like the others. She was here to stay.

With each of these huts there was a small attached bathroom with cemented floor. The provision of running water was still not there but there was a big drum of clear water with a lid for a cover, kept at a corner. A clean bucket and mug was also there for her use.

"*Ananya didi*, may I come in once?" a voice outside stopped Ananya just as she was about to close the bathroom door.

She opened the matted door of the hut to find Subal waiting outside. He was holding a bucket of steaming water in his left hand and a bunch of multi-colored season flowers in the other.

"Sister Kuhelika said you are not used to the cold water of the village, so I got warm water for your bath, otherwise you might catch a cold", Subal explained in one breath as he wriggled past Ananya to keep the bucket of hot water inside the bathroom.

"And this I got for you", he said with a smile as he handed the bunch of flowers to her.

Ananya felt too overwhelmed to speak.

"Kuhu was still her old self . . . . compassionate and full of concern" she thought.

Subal had already run out of the room.

"*Didi* take your bath before the water gets cold", he had warned before leaving.

Ananya closed the door and moved towards the desk. There was a crude, hand-made, bamboo vase placed on the table.

"Must be the handicraft of one of these ashramites", she guessed.

She carefully half-filled it with water and put the flowers in it.

Within seconds, her world was flooded with colors.

She thanked Subal silently.

When Ananya got ready and stepped out of her hut, it was 9.40. She was dressed in a lemon yellow salwar suit and her wet hair, lightly combed, hung limply from her shoulders. Without her regular lipstick, *bindi* or even ear and nose studs, she looked older than her real self.

"Sister kuhelika will meet you at the temple, come with me", Subal again came running from nowhere.

This time he was accompanied by two other boys, about his age, and a little girl.

"*Ananya didi*, this is Bolai, this is Anondo and this is Reema, they are my friends", Subal introduced them cheerfully.

"You can call them if I am not around", he said.

Ananya took out a few candies from the small bag she was carrying. Siddharth had given those to her in the station.

She handed out the candies to the children. Their faces instantly lit up and so was Ananya's heart.

On their way to the temple, which, she learnt, was at the other end of the compound, Ananya asked them where they would be going after reaching her.

All of them seemed to be dressed in a kind of uniform.

The boys were in khaki shorts and white shirts and the girl was in a white tunic.

"We will go to school, *didi*", Subal said.

"It is just by the temple" Bolai added.

"Yes, I guessed you all are going to school", Ananya said.

"When does it start?" she asked.

"Ten", this time the little girl chirped. Ananya was quite amused to notice that she had been holding on to her hand since the time she had given them the candies.

"Her innocent gesture of friendship", Ananya thought.

She didn't attempt to take away her hand.

"And when do you get over?" Ananya asked again.

"At four" Subal replied, "But in between we have our lunch—break from one o clock to two o clock".

"We eat and play during that time", It was Reema again.

"We all eat together in the temple courtyard", Anondo informed.

"Which classes are you all in?" Ananya wanted to know.

"We are in class eight and Reema is in six", Bolai replied.

In the course of the conversation Ananya did not realize that they had been walking for over ten minutes now.

She was almost in the sixth month of her pregnancy now and felt a little out of breath. However she walked religiously for an hour everyday, keeping Dr.Ghosh's advice in mind.

"You go inside *didi*, we will proceed to school", Subal told her as Ananya found herself standing in a wide stretch of open courtyard adjoining the temple.

Asking the children to carry on, Ananya moved towards the temple.

She did not need to go inside. Kuhu met her at the door.

"Are you facing any inconvenience?" genuine concern oozed from her voice.

"I have spoken to your Dr. Ghosh on the number you gave me. He has agreed to come down once a month to check you. He seems really fond of you", kuhu spoke in a quiet, assuring tone.

"For other emergencies I have kept the senior doctor of the nearest government—hospital, informed. He is a frequent visitor to this ashram."

"I will never forget all this, you have been an angel to me", Ananya's voice choked as she held her friend's hand firmly.

Words could never express how grateful she actually was.

"I have done nothing dear, it's all the doings of the Almighty, have faith," she said and smiled.

"You were talking about some surprise I remember", Ananya smiled back, wiping a drop of tear that hung from her eye.

"For that you have to come to the school with me and in any case I want you to see our school"

"Yes I am waiting to see it and when will I start teaching here?" Ananya enquired enthusiastically.

"You will, but not immediately. Dr. Ghosh has told me that you need to be in complete rest . . . . only light activities permitted", she smiled again.

"But Kuhu . . . . I am sorry, *Sister*, I told you I need to serve the ashram in some way, otherwise I cannot . . . ."

"Don't worry about all that", Sister Kuhelika interrupted.

"All that has been taken care of. You will be under no obligation in this ashram till you are ready to work."

"But who will bear my expenses for these few months and even after it, till I am ready?" Ananya asked, disturbed.

She was already so indebted to Kuhu that she didn't want to increase the burden of debt.

"What are friends for Ananya?" Her friend tried to appease her.

"But you are already doing enough for me!" Ananya protested.

"I am not talking about myself dear." She said.

"Then which friend are you talking about? Who is it that wants to take my responsibility and not even known to me?" Ananya demanded.

"How does anybody else here other than you, know me?"

"There is not one but two of them. I wrote to them about you." She said.

"You are testing my patience now Sister Kuhelika. Please tell me who they are. I want to meet them" Ananya pleaded.

"Both of them are abroad at present. I told you I wrote to them about you. So you can't meet them right now." She grinned, this time enjoying teasing her schoolmate.

"Trust me Ananya, they voluntarily offered to help . . . . they claimed they had that right . . . . one of them even wished to come down and take you with her. But I said you wouldn't agree and instead suggested this method of help." She continued.

"And what makes you think that I'll accept help from strangers?" Ananya asked.

"You will because you can't hurt them", Sister Kuhelika replied confidently.

"But why should I bother about how some strangers might feel?" Ananya sounded curious and impatient.

"When did I say they are *strangers* Ananya? I told you they are *friends*," she explained.

"Enough now! Please tell me; please please . . . . who are you talking about?"

"Katha and Sree." Sister Kuhelika finally said.

"What are you talking about?" Ananya stood stock still, completely taken aback.

"Why? Have you forgotten them? Or do you think they are strangers now? Sister Kuhelika asked.

"But how did you get in touch with them"? Ananya enquired.

"About seven years back Sree had come to Kolkata. She was looking for me. She got in touch with my mother and heard about me and this ashram. She had come to meet me. After going back to States she told everything to Katha. They live in the same city you see.

Since then both have been regular patrons of this ashram. In fact this school building has been built with the funds donated by them."

Ananya had been listening quietly all the while. She was too spellbound to speak.

"They kept enquiring about you in their letters", Sister kuhelika continued, "but I didn't know much about you. And none of us had any contact details of your parents. Had you not taken my number from my mother and called, we would never have met . . . . it's entirely the work of destiny you see".

"Hmmmm", Ananya let out a deep sigh.

It was like an old jig saw puzzle falling into place.

Pieces were taking their place to form a unified whole again.

Friends are angels, *friendship* is *religion*, She had heard someone say, long time back.

"Was this the surprise you were talking about?" Ananya asked.

She still couldn't believe that her long lost childhood friends, sitting so far away, separated for so many years, had come back to support her just when she needed them the most.

She closed her eyes to recollect their faces.

"No, there's something else, come with me", Sister Kuhelika beckoned her to follow. Ananya obeyed.

The school building was a simple double-storied structure.

Walking along the corridor of the first floor she thought of Katha and Sree's contribution to the ashram and her heart swelled with pride. She felt a painful longing to meet them.

"I shall write to them tonight, I need to thank them for everything", she decided.

"Ananya, this way", Sister Kuhelika motioned her to enter a room after the row of classrooms.

The classes had already started and the children were busy learning their lessons. A few curious eyes tried to see who it was walking away with Sister Kuhelika.

It was quite a big school, secondary level, and was affiliated to the State Board of Education. Most of the village children came here to study because the expenses were nominal.

Long time back, *guruji*, a native of the village, had taken upon himself the responsibility of educating the children of Madhabpur.

The ashram not only provided the students with free books and meals but also bore their medical expenses.

The orphans like Subal, Bolai, Anondo, Reema and others were inmates of the ashram itself.

Ananya followed Sister Kuhelika into a small room.

The look of it suggested that it served as a small library and reading room. There were two rows of high and low benches. An elderly lady with her back to them was seated on a low bench. She seemed lost in a book open in front of her

"There waits your surprise", Sister Kuhelika motioned towards the elderly lady.

"Who is she?" Ananya asked in a whisper.

"Go and find out yourself", came the reply.

With hesitant steps Ananya approached the lady, careful not to disturb her.

She turned once but Kuhu was not at the door. She had disappeared.

"So you have finally come, dear?" a very familiar voice out of her crowded memory startled Ananya. She froze in her place.

When the lady turned to face her, Ananya couldn't believe her eyes.

She still looked the same.

The thin, bony frame exuding love and warmth and commanding the same magical personality.

Age had only greyed her hairs, it couldn't make her stoop. The same intelligent eyes glittered with life and vitality. Time had failed to wreck her.

Too bewildered to react, Ananya only muttered, "Miss Mitra!"

It took her a few more seconds to accept the reality in front of her and she bent hurriedly to touch the feet of the teacher she always idolized, her teacher who was now in her seventies but vivacious as ever.

"You knew I was coming?" Ananya asked, astonished.

"Yes my dear, Sister Kuhelika told me everything about you. I was waiting for you Ananya."

Ananya fought hard to control her tears.

"So my little girl has grown up and is going to be a mother now?" Miss Mitra touched her chin affectionately.

Ananya couldn't control herself any longer. She threw herself in the arms of her teacher and broke down.

The latter didn't attempt to stop her. She let her relieve herself.

This girl had struggled a lot in life, she had been told and now in her worst crisis she was without her parents' support.

"May be this is why *You* had wanted me to spend my remaining days in this ashram, *Lord* . . . . this child needs a mother now more than anyone else", the old teacher thought.

That night sleep eluded Ananya for a long long time. Too many things had happened in too short a time for her to grasp.

"An over-doze of surprises", she thought and chuckled.

But one thing she felt for certain; if there was heaven anywhere on earth then for her it was right here, in this remote village called Madhabpur.

Chapter 18

Life in Paradise
Karunashram
Madhabpur

Paradise had indeed unfolded itself for Ananya.

She was soon popular with all the ashramites.

As always, she was most comfortable with the orphan children staying there and they reciprocated her love and warmth with equal enthusiasm.

Ananya had also kept the promise she had made to her children back home. She had duly informed Siddharth and Vivek about her well-being and asked them to convey the message to her parents.

"Their reaction is justified", she always reminded herself, "and I need to do my duty".

Ananya knew how worried her parents would be for her in spite of all their severity.

And now that she was going to be a mother herself, she felt the bond even more strongly.

Kuhu and Miss Mitra were over-protective about her.

Miss Mitra would personally supervise whether she took her food properly according to the doctor's prescription, whether she did her exercises regularly or whether she took her medicines in time.

Guruji had also developed a soft corner for this sweet-natured girl.

Often she would be summoned by *Guruji* along with some other inmates of the ashram, to the meditation hall and there he would read out excerpts from the *Bhagwad Gita* and explain its significance.

He taught in a simple, lucid manner, comprehensible to all, and Ananya enjoyed those sessions immensely.

The kind of mental strength she had developed here was to stand her in good stead in the years to come.

Ananya was indebted to *Guruji's* lessons on life, for all this.

Now it was easy to understand how Kuhu had become a tower of strength over the years.

Guruji was a great spiritual guide, a believer in action and not words, a noble soul, truly dedicated to the service of humanity.

Like every other inmate of the ashram, Ananya also respected him immensely.

She enjoyed most the meditation sessions under *guruji's* guidance. Particularly those, in which he would teach them to control anger, develop patience and inculcate tolerance.

As the months advanced, the whole ashram was excited about Ananya's baby. Everybody was busy doing his or her bit to make the occasion special.

The children maintained the garden outside her hut immaculately.

Subal never forgot to keep fresh flowers in her room everyday.

But by now he knew that *Ananya didi's* favourite were white lilies.

Kuhu had cut out from old calendars and hung a number of pictures of sweet faces of children all around her room.

Miss Mitra doted on her like a pampering mother.

The girls in the ashram had started stitching clothes for the new—born and on knowing that the baby was due in October, they had started knitting little sweaters, socks and mittens.

Ananya was not allowed to do any work, and everyone in the ashram, old or young, literally pampered her. Ananya had become the darling of everyone.

In the monsoon months when she could no longer stroll outside, they would all gather in the common sitting room and play *antakshari*, *ludo* or listen to stories from Miss Mitra.

She was a never-ending source of entertainment and hence was favourite of everyone here also as she used to be in the school.

Electricity was yet to reach the ashram though the telephone connection had come. But they were expecting it before the pujas as had been earlier promised by the authorities.

Kuhu had been relentlessly corresponding with the local political party leaders to get it done. The ashram had deposited the necessary money and done the needful on its part, the execution from the electricity board was only awaited.

It was the first time a new—life would be born in the ashram and Sister Kuhelika didn't want the baby to be born in darkness.

To Ananya all this didn't matter.

Everyone in this place had illuminated her life so brightly that she didn't mind the other darkness. The love and affection they showered on her had been more than enough compensation for all that she had to lose or leave behind.

There was only one deep—buried pain that shot to the surface and tormented her. She guarded it carefully from everyone. But as the days advanced, a face from the past haunted her more and more. Worst of all she experienced a longing that she had abandoned long time back. She craved to see once that man . . . . the man she had loved . . . . the father of her child.

"Samarth!"

She would often utter the name in the privacy of her room wrapped in shadowed darkness, as she stared at his photograph, the only one she carried with her, in the dim, flickering light of the oil—lamp.

Chapter 19

Birth–Death–Rebirth
Karunashram
Madhabpur
6ᵗʰ October, 1997

It was just as she was about to take her bath in the morning, Ananya felt the first stabbing pain that for a while blinded her.

Her delivery was due any moment and she was prepared for it.

"Let the worst be over as soon as possible", was what she had been wishing for over a month now.

To carry such an abnormally swollen belly for so long was not only cumbersome but also awkward.

"Hold it sweetheart . . . . we have almost made it . . . . soon we will be together", she would say addressing her womb, every time she felt them kicking her belly from inside, as if in a hurry to be born.

She didn't mind the pain.

"That's the call of my child, my baby", she would tell herself and feel overwhelmed with pride and joy.

This was a unique experience, almost divine, to feel her baby grow inside her bit by bit everyday, and with that her tie strengthening with a new life, yet to see the light of the world.

Ananya staggered back to her bed.

It was an incising pain, increasing now with every passing moment.

"Subaa . . . . l, Reemaaaa", she shouted as she dragged her heavy self towards the door to unlatch it.

Even though the distance from her bed to the door was hardly a few steps, Ananya felt herself panting for breath.

"*Ananya didi* what happened? Are you all right?"

The nervous voice was of Dipti, an inmate of karunashram.

"Subal, Reema, Bolai have all gone to the big pond of the Mukherjee's, just outside the ashram. The children, I heard are having a swimming competition there today", Dipti explained as she helped Ananya from out of the chair she had planted herself on, to her bed.

"Dipti, call Sister Kuhelika and Miss Mitra . . . . fast", Ananya said, gasping in pain.

It was now that Dipti noticed how profusely Ananya was sweating away.

"One minute *didi*, I'll just be back", said Dipti as she stormed out of the room.

During the next few minutes, Ananya felt the world around her darkening. The pain was now unbearable. It was nothing like she had ever experienced before.

"Am I dying?" for the first time in the course of her pregnancy Ananya felt scared.

When Sister Kuhelika, Miss Mitra, Dipti and two other girls came running into Ananya's room, they found her grimacing in pain.

"Sister Kuhelika, send for the ambulance . . . . Quick", Miss Mitra shouted as she tried to wipe away the sweat from Ananya's face and fan her with a hand-made, palm-leaf fan.

Dipti rushed to the office room to telephone the Madhabpur General Hospital, for the ambulance.

"They just have one ambulance for the entire village . . . I just hope its available", Sister Kuhelika sounded apprehensive.

"But the ambulance was donated by our ashram sister, they have to send it when we need it", Aruna said.

"The ashram does not make donations on any condition Aruna, whatever we do, we do for the benefit of the entire village", Sister Kuhelika corrected her.

After another twenty minutes when Ananya was being carried to the ambulance on the stretcher, she was wet, perspiring all over, tears had moistened her pale face and the lips that had been bitten hard to stop herself from yelling in pain, looked blue-black. She felt something ripping her apart and she tried to pray to have enough strength to bear it all.

Madhabpur General Hospital was a hospital in name only. The government aid that the hospital was entitled to, never came and whatever little did come in at times, hardly met up any requirement. The hospital was ill-equipped, worse maintained and the condition of the only operation theatre was pathetic. Medicines were almost always out of stock. Perhaps it was taken for granted that the people of Madhabpur will never require anything more than what was available to them. Some initial pleas for reform, in the beginning, fell in deaf ears and then everyone stopped complaining also. The villagers felt obliged that they had this much medical facility whereas many of the neighbouring villages, they had heard, had not even a clinic or a dispensary.

Whatever little the 3 doctors, 2 nurses along with 1 attendant and 1 sweeper could do for the patients, was to a large extent due to the donations in cash and kind that came from *karunashram* from time to time.

Sometimes the girls from the ashram came in to offer services when all the 20 beds remained full and the doctors and nurses failed to cope with the pressure.

So when a patient was coming to the hospital from the ashram, the entire hospital staff felt only too obliged to offer the best that they could.

Almost immediately on reaching the hospital, a doctor and two nurses started attending Ananya.

"You all please wait here", the younger of the two nurses requested, motioning Sister Kuhelika, Miss Mitra, Dipti, Aruna And Neeti to the bench in the corridor, as Ananya was hurried on to the labour room.

"Doctor . . . . how long will it be? I can't take it anymore", Ananya was sobbing beyond control now.

"Relax Ananya, it wont be very long dear . . . . you are already in severe labor, so it should be easy", the elderly doctor assured in a kind tone.

When the nurse prepared her for the delivery, Ananya thought she won't survive to see her child.

The pain was tearing her apart, she screamed in agony as she heard some voices urging her *"push, push, push harder Ananya . . . . just a little more"* and she tried to obey with the last bit of strength left in her . . . .

Miles away in Guwahati, a party was going on in full swing in an apartment on the first floor of Riddhi Towers residential complex, at Navinnagar. It was a day—party to enable the participation of a special guest, Rajni Behl, who was flying out of town that evening.

Rajni Behl, the celebrated journalist, was to fly abroad the next day from Delhi. She had postponed her journey to Delhi till the evening to attend the engagement of her beloved cousin to one of her dearest friends. It was through her that the couple had met and they refused to celebrate without her.

Rajni couldn't commit that she would be able to attend their wedding few months later, and so the engagement was preponed to ensure her presence.

Almost the entire media circle of the city was present to cheer the once-upon-a-time, talk-of-the-town affair finally reaching its goal. They were all here to congratulate Samarth Bose and Priya Sharma, on their engagement.

Ananya couldn't recollect when exactly the hell had been over for her. All she remembered was a last surge of searing pain while something slipped out of her body and she fell unconscious.

"It was worse than a nightmare . . . . and a never-ending one", Ananya thought, trying to open her eyes which felt very heavy.

She felt a nurse tending to her. She tried to move a little but cried out in pain.

"Move slowly, the stitches are fresh so they are hurting . . . it'll heal soon", the nurse said smiling.

"Its still lot less than the delivery pain", Ananya said weakly.

"My baby?" She suddenly seemed to remember and looked around expectantly.

She saw the blurred faces of Kuhu, Miss Mitra, the girls and even Subal, Bolai, Reema and Anondo.

"It's not a baby Ananya", Sister Kuhelika said.

Ananya's heart sank. "Why? Did anything go wrong? Please tell me, please", she pleaded.

"No no you foolish girl, I mean to say that you have babies . . . . you had twins Ananya, a boy and a girl", Sister Kuhelika said with uncharacteristic excitement that took everyone by surprise.

She held the hand of her friend warmly as Miss Mitra kept hers on Ananya's forehead.

Tears of joy, relief and gratitude rolled down her cheeks and Ananya thanked God from the depths of her soul.

"Your son was born at 11.17 and your daughter followed a minute later . . . it was a smooth delivery", the attending nurse said.

"When can I see them?" Ananya asked impatiently.

"Very Soon", she promised, "the doctors are checking them", she said.

"Is everything fine?" Ananya asked with typical motherly concern.

"Yes yes Ananya . . . everything is perfect", this time one of the two doctors who just walked in holding one of the new-borns, replied, assuring her. This elderly doctor was followed by his assistant who held the other baby.

"Have you thought about their names?" the junior doctor asked, smiling.

"She had certainly thought of two names but didn't know that both would be required", the senior doctor joked and everyone laughed.

They were right. Ananya had already decided on the names.

Looking down on the cradle beside her she saw her children for the first time and was swept over by a rush of affection and tenderness hitherto unknown to her.

"My children!" she couldn't believe it. It was the first time she was looking at new-born babies and to think they were her own! It was an overpowering sensation.

"She touched them tenderly", careful not to hurt them. They were so small and helpless.

"I'll call them Piyal and Pihu", she said.

To herself Ananya said quietly, "I am reborn today".

In his apartment at Riddhi Towers in Guwahati, the clock showed 11.17 when Samarth Bose slipped an old but carefully preserved diamond ring on the ring-finger of his fiancée Priya Sharma, to a loud burst of applause and cheers from those present.

Chapter 20

The Revelation
Guwahati
6th October, 1997

When the last guest left his house, it was almost 5 by his watch. Samarth felt exhausted. Blasting music for the last few hours was making his head throb. Rajni and Priya were the last to leave. They had stayed back to wait for Priya's parents to call.

Her parents were settled in Texas with her brother and they wished to congratulate and bless the couple together, over the phone.

"We would all be there for the wedding, well in advance", Priya's father had said.

"We missed sir", Samarth had responded with perfect courtesy.

"Samarth, my daughter is a hot-head, may be a little pampered you see, but she is not bad at heart and she went back to India only for you. Please bear with her, she'll be a good wife I assure you", her mother had said in a voice that echoed concern and sincerity.

"You don't worry about all that aunty, I'll take care of everything", Samarth had assured her honestly.

"Thank you so much son, and god bless you both", she said with relief.

Rajni was moving to the airport straight from his house and Priya was accompanying her.

"I'll join you", Samarth had offered.

But Priya insisted that he stayed back to rest. Samarth had already been complaining about a nagging headache for some time.

"She has already begun to change, she is beginning to understand", Samarth thought.

"Do you need help *dada*?"

Samarth turned and saw Ishita had walked into the drawing room. She offered to help seeing him busy tiding up things.

"There is nothing much to do. Just these plates need to be taken away and the CDs need to be put back in the shelf", he replied.

"You go and change, I'll do it", Ishita said.

"*Dada* why didn't JC come?" Ishita asked, as she gathered up the plates.

"He had called up to say he got stuck up at the last moment", Samarth lied. "He is hardly free these days", he tried to explain but did not sound too convincing.

"Still, I mean, he is your best friend, he could have accommodated . . . . it was your special occasion", she argued.

"Why do you have to be so critical about everything Ishu? And stop making an issue out of it", Samath sounded irritated.

"I don't intend to make any issue out of anything", Ishita snapped back, "It was *ma* who was asking me . . . I was just repeating her. Anyway who cares, you always follow your own will", she stormed out of the room.

Samarth had himself been tormented throughout the day by JC's absence.

"He had promised to come, but why didn't he call up once to inform that he can't make it?" Samarth wondered.

"*Ma* also noticed it", Samarth thought, "But most of the time she was in her room".

Prabha had always been a friendly and non-interfering mother. She was quite popular with the friends of all her children. They spoke to her freely on any subject including their love affairs and secret crushes. Most of them were addicted to the mouth-watering snacks she made for them. The best thing about her was that she never mind an untimely guest and warmly welcomed anybody from family or from her children's friend circle at any time of the day. Even at sixty two she was a store house of energy.

"Surprisingly *ma* never seemed very comfortable with Priya", samarth reflected.

But Prabha had never uttered any disapproval regarding her son's choice. She had always accepted the decision of her children without any objection. They were all grown up now and she had full faith in them.

"*Ma* is never her usual self when it comes to Priya" samarth had noticed.

"She looks restrained and withdrawn. Is there a problem? Why doesn't she speak it out?" Samarth had often wondered, frustrated.

"May be she finds the language difference a barrier", Samarth tried to reason out.

"Priya still can't speak Bengali though she understands slightly . . . . she needs time and then in course of time things will straighten out", Samarth assured himself.

He was planning to take a pill for headache and go off to sleep for a couple of hours but before that wanted to try JC's number just once more. Since morning he had dialed his number at least forty times but there had been no response.

"Is he avoiding me by any chance?" Samarth couldn't help wondering. But the next moment he felt JC could never do such a thing with him.

Suddenly Samarth had a desperate urge to meet his best pal. "What is wrong? I have to find out", he resolved.

It was almost seven by the time he reached his friend's house. The flat adjacent his was occupied by his cousin and his wife.

"In case I don't get to meet him I'll leave a message with *Bhaia* and *bhabi*", Samarth decided while taking the elevator to JC's first floor flat at Ulubari.

He had to wait for more than a couple of minutes after ringing the door-bell and wondered whether anyone was inside. Finally when JC came and opened the door, Samarth didn't have the heart to demand any explanation from him.

It seemed he had been sleeping. His eyes were swollen and red as though from over-sleep and he looked very dejected if not sick.

"Are you okay?" Samarth asked as he stepped in. The concern in his voice did not go unnoticed by his friend.

"I am fine, don't worry. You tell me what brings you here today?" JC asked in an uncharacteristic cold voice.

"Why? Can't I drop in without a reason, just like that?" Samarth asked, hurt.

"No I thought it's your big day today and you should be busy elsewhere", JC replied, pouring himself a glass of water.

"Oh! So you remembered it was my big day today?" Samarth couldn't control the sarcasm in his voice this time.

"There was no reason to forget it", came the cold response.

"Then why didn't you come?" Samarth demanded.

JC remained silent.

"Why didn't you take my calls? I called at least . . . ."

"I didn't feel like", JC interrupted.

The blunt reply shocked Samarth.

"Come again", he said.

"Yes you heard me correct, I didn't attend your engagement or take your calls because I didn't feel like", JC said in an impassioned tone.

Samarth thought he was not sitting with his childhood friend whom he knew like the back of his hand. It was some stranger that he was talking to.

"May I know the reason behind this indifference?" Samarth asked bitterly. He was hurt, terribly hurt at JC's attitude but he wanted to get to the root of it.

"Is it necessary to make me talk Sam? It would only embitter our relationship. Better we both stay quiet about it. Certain issues in life should be left like that", JC said in the same cold tone.

"Still you say. I want to hear it, I want to know what happened suddenly that has created a rift between us . . . . something I thought was never possible", Samarth demanded angrily.

"Well if you insist then hear it", JC said. "I don't like that *pretty doll* you have chosen for your life partner, I never thought her to be a suitable match for you".

"Are you talking about Priya?" Samarth asked in disbelief.

He had never heard his friend talk so critically about anyone.

"Who else?" this time the disgust in JC's voice was unconcealed.

"But why JC?" Samarth could barely speak.

"I never felt she would be a home-maker, I find her too self-centered . . . . she would never be the right woman for a family loving man like you", JC replied.

"But you know that she has forsaken a bright career abroad just for me?" Samarth argued desperately.

"That is it Sam. She has compromised too much for you and I'm afraid when the time comes she'll demand too much of a price for it. I just hope you are able to afford it then".

Silence followed for the next couple of minutes. Too much had been asked and said.

"Sam just excuse me for sometime, I need to freshen up", JC said as he stood up and walked towards the washroom.

Samarth remained seated in the drawing room and flipped through morning paper but he could not read anything. He was too disturbed to concentrate on anything right now.

A few minutes later JC's mobile phone, lying on the center-table rang.

"Your phone is ringing", Samarth shouted, "looks like an out-station number, will you take it?" he asked.

"I can't come out just now, you receive the call and take the message", JC shouted back.

"Hello", Samarth answered.

"Hello JC this is Sister Kuhelika from Madhabpur", a female voice spoke from the other side.

"Sorry ma'am JC is not here at the moment. I am his friend, you can leave a message for him if you wish or I'll ask him to call you back", Samarth replied.

"Please tell him that I had called up to give good news. His sister Ananya has given birth to two beautiful twins this morning. They are all fine and she wishes to see her brother once."

When JC came out of the washroom, he found Samarth, sitting on the sofa, wearing a peculiar expression, the mobile phone still clutched in his hand. His face was ashen and he seemed completely lost.

"Samarth, whose call was it?" JC asked.

There was no reply. Samarth didn't appear to have heard him.

"Samarth", JC called out again and stretched his hand for the phone.

"You knew about it all through and still you didn't tell me?" Samarth's question took his friend by surprise.

"What are you talking about?" he asked.

"*This*", Samarth said, extending the phone, he was almost sobbing now.

When JC checked the number the call had come from, he knew that the secret was out.

"What did they say?" he asked quietly.

"*My children* JC, Ananya has given birth to our children today and their father doesn't even have the right to know about it", Samarth broke into uncontrollable sobs now. "Why didn't you tell me before, why?"

JC was hugging his friend very tight now. He found it difficult to fight back his own emotions.

"I was helpless Sam, believe me, she had made me swear", he tried to explain guiltily.

127

"*That's my Ananya JC, that's my Aan*, she punished me this way. She wanted me to have the heaven and chose hell for herself . . . . that's the way she punished me", Samarth wept.

Chapter 21

Lonely in the Crowd
Karunashram
Madhabpur
October–December, 2007.

Sister Kuhelika's relentless endeavor had paid off. When Ananya returned to the ashram after a week, the entire *karunashram* glittered with glowing electric bulbs.

She was deliberately brought back in the evening to enable the ashramites give her a literally bright welcome.

Piyal and Pihu stepped into a world of light.

Guruji waited at the door to bless her and the children. He had arranged for a special *puja* that evening.

Ananya was overwhelmed to find Dr. Ghosh waiting for her as well.

"He came down this morning Ananya when he was informed that you are coming back this evening", *Guruji* explained.

"The mother and the children, all look fit and fine", he observed, smiling.

Piyal was in Miss Mitra's lap and Pihu in Dipti's. Ananya bent down to touch the feet of *Guruji*, Dr.Ghosh and her teacher.

They all blessed her from the core of their hearts.

Amidst all the joys and celebrations, Ananya couldn't help missing her parents. Her heart was silently crying for them.

"Only if they had blessed my children once", she wished.

Their thought brought a lump in her throat which she tried to swallow down quickly.

At this time of the year there was a nip in the evening air.

Ananya wrapped a thin shawl around her as she sat down to reply Katha and Sree's letters. They had been in constant touch to find out how things had been going with her.

"I can never repay their debts in this lifetime", Ananya thought.

Piyal and Pihu were in Dipti and Aruna's care. They were both struggling to put the twins off to sleep.

The ashram always came alive at this time. The Durga Puja was just a week away and the young and old were all busy making the preparations. The birth of the twins had added to the enthusiasm of one and all.

The autumn sun was the harbinger of the pujas. The blue sky stretched overhead with small tufts of clouds sailing across it. The air laden with the fragrance of *shiuli* and the swaying white stalks of the *kaash* plants at the distance made Ananya unusually contemplative.

It was the morning of *Mahasaptami* and the sound of the *dhaak* being beaten in the temple premises carried her heart far, far away to the days of her childhood.

Special dishes prepared by mom, new clothes, sweets, visiting relatives and friends and pandal hopping with dad. Ananya's heart wrung.

She suddenly felt lonely, very, very lonely.

"*Guruji* is calling you to the office *Didi*", Reema had come running to inform.

"Ok I am coming", Ananya said.

Pihu was on her lap. She carefully buttoned up her sweater and walked towards the office-room. Piyal was in the care of Miss Mitra.

"Come in Ananya", *Guruji* said when she appeared at the door.

"Your brother had called up, he said he would call in another five minutes or so".

Ananya felt a quiver. Finally *bhai* had called. She had been waiting for this call. She had been wondering why his call didn't come. Ananya pulled up a chair and sat carefully with her daughter.

The phone rang almost immediately.

Guruji picked it up and then passed it to Ananya.

He then took the infant from her and slowly moved towards the door, affectionately lisping away strange words to the delicate child in his arms.

"Hello", Ananya found her voice unsteady.

"Hello *sis*", the familiar voice of JC floated in from the other side.

Ananya's voice was too choked with emotions to speak. Still she forced out "why did you take so long to call?"

Her hurt voice pained her brother.

"I'm sorry *sis* but let me congratulate you first", he said, trying to sound normal.

"I call them Piyal and Pihu . . . . You know they are twins", ananya tried to sound cheerful.

"Yes yes dear, Sister Kuhelika said so and I can't tell you how happy I am. I'll soon come to see them", he said.

Ananya couldn't believe her ears, "are you serious *bhai*?" she asked.

"Of course I am, in fact had it not been for some professional commitments, I would have come over during the *pujas* only", he said.

"When will you come?" Ananya asked expectantly.

"I hope to be free around the first week of December but won't commit anything now. Trust me *sis* I am myself dying to see the children", he said.

"I know *bhai*', Ananya replied honestly, "I'll wait for you" she said before replacing the receiver.

None spoke about Samarth, though both wanted to.

Chapter 22

The Rendezvous
Guwahati
October, 1997

"You can't be serious Sam", Priya said in shocked amazement as she stared at Samarth's outstretched palm in front of her. There was a gold band studded with an exquisite sapphire.

It was the ring Priya had given Samarth on their engagement. She had chosen it keeping in mind that sapphire was Samarth's birth-stone.

"I'm serious Priya, but I'm helpless, I'm breaking this engagement".

The cold bluntness, with which he uttered the words, shoved her back to her senses.

Earlier in the evening Samarth had called her up to say that he needed to meet her urgently. But this was the last thing she had expected.

When Samarth started talking about Ananya, Priya had felt bad . . . . not because he had an affair with her but because he had kept it from her so long.

"Two years is a long time and even I lived pretty fast for sometime and it had been fun", Priya had tried to reason with herself.

But breaking the engagement was nothing like what she had been prepared for. This was serious relationship that they were into and now the families were involved too.

"Listen Sam, don't be an emotional fool as you have always been", Priya tried to make her fiancée see reason.

"These kind of passing affairs happen when you are young, single and living a dynamic life. It happened with me also but that doesn't mean we have to be serious about them all . . . . we can't tie knots with everyone darling, can we? So stop being stupid. It's all our past and it's all over. Let's look forward to the future now", Priya tried to remain levelheaded suppressing her seething temper.

"She is not *just everyone* Priya and she was *never* a casual affair in my life."

"Oh I see. Then who is *she* that suddenly ignites your sense of moral responsibility?" Priya asked bitterly.

"She is the mother of my children Priya and she is the woman I choose to call my wife", Samarth's voice did not falter even once as he spoke.

He felt a strange kind of confidence, something he never thought himself capable of.

"What?" Priya spat out this time.

"You guys went that far?" her notorious anger was surfacing itself, disbelief still lingering in her voice.

Samarth nodded silently.

"And what the hell had you been doing with me Mr. Samarth Bose? You were playing some kind of game or were you trying to avenge what I had done to you two years back?" Priya was shouting now.

"No Priya its nothing like that, you please calm down, I'll explain", Samarth held on to his cool.

"Calm down? You expect me to calmdown after hearing all this? Oh my God, such a cheating! Such a crook behind that naïve face!"

Priya was pacing up and down the room now. In spite of the chill in the air at this time of the year, she was sweating. Her fair face flushed red.

"You have any idea how I might be feeling now?" Samarth thought he heard a streak of pain in Priya's voice.

"Yes I know. I have been through it myself, you are forgetting", he said.

"Yes I knew it, I knew it was your revenge. Your bloody male ego was hurt two years back and you thought this would be the perfect way to level scores . . . . You are disgusting Samarth", Priya was howling in anger and humiliation.

"You have every right to say anything you wish Priya. The mistake is mine and I am prepared to take responsibility for all this", Samarth said honestly.

"That doesn't make my situation any better Sam, how do you intend to make up for the social disgrace that my family and I would be going through?" she barked.

"I am prepared to apologize publicly, if you so want", Samarth said.

"I sacrificed everything I ever wanted, for *you* Sam".

"Yeah I know. And Ananya sacrificed *me* so that I could have everything I had wanted", Samarth said quietly.

"Then what made you leave that great lady? Why the hell did you come back to me?" Priya demanded sarcastically.

"It was you who came back to me Priya. I had never left you. If I left anyone, it was Ananya", Samarth reminded her.

"Yes I know and that was the biggest mistake of my life. You know Samarth, you don't deserve anyone, neither me, nor Ananya. You are a pathetic coward", Priya said maliciously.

"I certainly don't deserve Ananya. As for you, you will bless me someday for backing out of your life. Our priorities were always different Priya. You would have regretted throughout your life for having to sacrifice your dreams and I wouldn't have been able to take that for long", Samarth paused.

"Good excuse Sam but where was this wisdom when you reciprocated my feelings?" Priya lashed out again.

"The wisdom was always there but perhaps as you pointed out, I was a coward then. But thank god, before ruining so many lives I managed to muster up my courage. I made a mistake in the first place letting Ananya go and I made the second mistake when I let you come in my life again. I admit I got carried away but believe me if possible that I didn't do anything intentionally. My mistakes are grave ones Priya but I am not a criminal."

Priya sat down on the sofa opposite Samarth. For the first time in the course of the turbulent evening, she appeared a little calm.

"Why did you leave Ananya and why have you decided to go back to her? Is it for her children?" She asked.

"Our children", Samarth corrected her.

"No Priya, she never called me back. I am not even sure if she'll accept me back but I want to try at least once to go to her and tell her how much I love her", Samarth's voice was choked.

"And what was it that you felt for me so long?" Priya asked.

"I guess I was carried away by your beauty, your glamour, your charm . . . . everything", Samarth replied honestly.

"And today these things don't appeal to you anymore?" Priya asked.

"They do but they appeal only to my senses not to my heart", came the reply.

"So its *love* that's taking you back to her?" Priya wanted to know.

"A little more than that. My respect for her values, my regards for her courage, my adoration for her self-esteem and above all my gratitude for teaching me what it means to love . . . . all this is taking me back to her", Samarth confessed sincerely.

A long silence followed.

Finally Samarth stood up and moved towards the door.

"I'm really sorry Priya. Forgive me if you can", he uttered.

"Just a moment Samarth", Priya's voice made him turn from the door and face her.

"You were forgetting this", she held out the diamond ring, "perhaps it refused to be with me because I had once refused to wear it", she said.

There was no mistaking the anguish in her voice. But Samarth fought back his urge to console or comfort her.

"It would only make things difficult", he thought.

"All the best Sam", Priya was crying for the first time, "but I'll never forgive you, never", she muttered as she closed the door on him forever.

When Samarth stepped out on the road, the cool October breeze welcomed him with a soothing touch.

"It's never easy to hurt anyone", he thought.

But strangely he didn't regret all that had happened. He did not even feel that he had lost anything. If there was any regret it was that he had to hurt Priya who had to pay the price of his mistake.

"It was a *rendezvous*", Samarth thought while walking down the road, "with myself", and suddenly he felt very happy, very free.

He wanted to run.

He felt like a man who had just been liberated of the shackles of confusion and cowardice that had bound him so long.

Samarth was reborn. And this Samarth had the courage to accept himself, to own up his weaknesses and was prepared to rectify them. This was an enlightened man.

Samarth didn't realize he had actually started running down the road, least bothered about the curious glances of the other pedestrians.

He was in a hurry. He had already wasted a lot of time. He was in a hurry now to run back home . . . . back to his *Ananya* and their children.

Chapter 23

The Call of the Past
Karunashram
Madhabpur
6ᵗʰ Dec, 1997

Ananya's excitement had been growing in leaps and bounds since morning. Even last night passed wsithout sleep. She had been waiting impatiently for the day-break.

Her little hut was prim and proper, fresh flowers bloomed in the vase and the soft winter sun hugged the room warmly.

Subal had worked hard with his friends to maintain the garden outside Ananya's hut. She admired it silently.

The twins were still fast asleep in their respective cradles. Ananya touched them tenderly. They had made up for all the hardships she had to go through.

"They are worth all that I had to stake or lose", she thought. "It feels so divine to be a mother, only if I could share it with you *ma*", she silently regretted.

But this morning was very special. Her children were two months old today and they were to have a very special visitor.

Ananya had been dying to meet this man ever since the birth of her children. And finally the day had come.

He was on his way. He had called up to inform that he had reached Kolkata the previous evening and an hour back he informed them again to say that he had boarded the train to Madhabpur.

Ananya was waiting. Waiting for JC to come.

She wanted to go to the station and receive her brother personally. But the trains on this route were never on time and Piyal and Pihu had to be fed once they woke up. So it would be Subal and Anondo who would go to bring the guest.

It was well past midday when the bouncy, old ambassador screeched to a halt in front of the ashram gate.

Ananya was inside her room, struggling to pacify a screaming Pihu.

"*Sister*", a deep voice from the door made her swing back instantly. She was still holding the child, rocking her in her arms.

"*Bhai*!" she uttered, half smiling, half crying.

Ananya hastened to the door to greet him.

JC embraced the mother with her child fondly.

"Where's the other little devil?" he asked cheerfully and then walking up to the cradle tried to pick up the other infant carefully but didn't.

"Oh I haven't washed yet, he might get an infection", he said.

"Hmmm, a responsible uncle I see", Ananya responded, smiling.

"I'm more responsible than you can imagine *sis*", something in JC's voice made Ananya curious.

He read the quizzical look in her eyes.

"I mean I haven't forgotten a brother's and an uncle's responsibility", JC said smiling.

"How can I see my sister after such a long time and meet the kids for the first time, without a present for you all?" he asked affectionately.

"Oh come on *bhai*," Ananya protested mildly. "It's enough for me and the children that you have come", she said sincerely.

Piyal was still fast asleep in his cradle and Pihu had finally become quiet. A moment's silence followed.

"Don't you want to know anything about Samarth?"

JC's point blank question caught Ananya off guard and she felt a shudder through her. How could she explain that she had been fighting the urge to do so for the last few minutes?

But she chose to remain silent.

"You don't have to hide your feelings from me *sis*," JC said with genuine affection.

"We can talk about all that later *bhai*, first you freshen up. Come I'll show you to your room", Ananya hurriedly tried to change the topic but he was persistent.

"Tell me Aan, will you never forgive Samarth?" he asked.

"You must be very tired after the journey. The local trains in this route are horrible. Would you take a shower now or should I get you a cup of tea first?" she asked

The big man rose from the wooden chair he was seated on and came near the bed where Ananya was sitting.

He sat down beside her quietly.

"Look at me Aan", he said.

Ananya turned to face him, eyes still downcast.

"I said look at me", he repeated.

Ananya looked up. Her gaze was held by his and she felt this man was reading all that was carefully suppressed in her heart.

"Let me get your tea," she stood up.

JC pulled her hand and forced her to sit down. "I want an answer Aan", he said.

"How does all that matter anymore *bhai*?" There was no mistaking the pain in her voice.

"It does sister, it does", the insistence in his voice surprised Ananya.

"I told you I will never buy my love at the cost of anybody's guilt or sympathy. So no question of forgiving anyone arises", this time she replied firmly.

"Have you thought about the children, their future?" He asked persuasively.

"The children are mine", Ananya shot back. "They are the result of my love and my faith and I can take care of them", she said firmly.

"But *sis* . . . ."

"There's no if or but *bhai*", Ananya interrupted him. "I know the world will call me foolish for all that has happened but I am still proud of myself *bhai* . . . ." She paused a while and said, "at least I am neither a coward,nor an escapist. If I made a mistake, I had the guts to bear the consequences and trust me *bhai*, there will never be a dearth of courage in me".

"But if Samarth wants to come back to you, then?"

"I told you *bhai*, nobody's pity is acceptable to me. I can't think of my children having a father who accepts them just because he feels guilty for having brought them to this world or because he tries to compensate for the wrong he had done to their mother. I am sure my children wouldn't like it either."

Ananya stood up and started moving towards the door.

"I'll get your tea", she said.

"What if Samarth really loves you and wants you back just because he loves you?"

Ananya swung back from the door.

"Why are you advocating so much for him *bhai*? I thought you had come to meet me and the children!" This time she couldn't hide the bitterness in her voice.

"*Didi*", subal's voice made her turn to the door again.

"Sister Kuhelika is asking if your lunch should be served here or you will join us all."

"No no we'll all eat together", JC promptly reply as he came towards the door.

"Then don't waste anymore time, go and have your shower first, we can talk later" Ananya said and then turning to Subal she instructed, "show him to his hut and get him some warm water for bath".

"I have already done that *didi*. The other *dada* must have freshened up by now. I had kept two buckets of hot water for them".

"*Other dada*?" Ananya asked, surprised.

"Who else has come with you *bhai*? You never told me so long?" but before she could complete her question JC was already following Subal to the guest-hut.

It was almost 1.30 now. "Everybody must be waiting for us at lunch", thought Ananya. According to ashram rules, normally they finished eating by 1 o clock but today probably they were being lenient for the guests.

"But who's accompanying JC?" she felt bitten by curiosity.

The afternoon sun felt comfortable. Here in the village it was quite cold even in this early December. Most of the trees around had shorn their leaves; few were beginning to get new ones. But the gardens before every hut looked very bright and colourful.

"Thanks to the children", Ananya thought, pleased at their effort. The dahlias had come out big and beautiful already, though still not in their full bloom.

"Hey *sis*, I am ready", JC waved at her from a distance.

He looked fresh now and comfortable in a pair of white *kurta pyjama*. But he was coming alone.

"Where is his companion?" Ananya wondered.

JC seemed to sense her question.

"My friend has already finished his lunch with the children. Subal told me he is in *guruji's* room, talking to him", he explained as they proceeded to the temple courtyard where everyone ate together.

JC was instantly popular with every ashramite. His easy, suave manners, endearing personality and lively sense of humour won everybody's heart. Miss Mitra took to immediate affection for this young man from the north-east and even the usually reserved sister Kuhelika broke into laughter quite a few times on hearing his anecdotes.

Lunch that afternoon at *karunashram* was an enjoyable experience.

Nobody spoke about the other guest.

After lunch Ananya decided to take JC to the school.

They were just about to proceed when Aruna who had been taking care of the children came and informed that *guruji* wanted Ananya in his room. He had sent for her.

"Did you leave the children alone in the room?" she asked, concerned.

"No" she said and then pointing to JC continued to say "his friend came and said he'll be there with the children for sometime, so I came here to inform you. But I am going back now" she turned to leave and again came back.

"*Didi*, Piyal is refusing to drink water . . . I tried my best but he is taking his mouth away from the feeding bottle, you please come back fast".

"Yes, I will but you please go back to them immediately", she said, not at all liking the idea that her babies should be lying in the care of some stranger. Aruna hurried away.

Turning to JC she said, "you go and rest for a while *bhai*, the journey must have been tiring. We'll go for a stroll in the evening and yes," she added, "call back your friend also, he must be tired too. I'll meet him in the evening."

"All right", he agreed.

Everyone returned to the respective works after lunch. The children were back to school along with Miss Mitra andSister Kuhelika, the elder girls went back to resume their stitching, basket-weaving and pot-making and JC was on his way back to the guest-hut.

Ananya headed for *guruji's* room. All the way she had a disturbing sensation about the stranger who had come with JC.

"Who is he?" she couldn't help wondering.

Chapter 24

Sam and Aan

"Yes come in Ananya", *guruji* said as Ananya softly knocked on the half-closed door of his hut.

"I heard, you sent for me *guruji*?" she asked.

"Yes I did Ananya, you sit down first", he said, raising his face from the biography of *Thakur Omkarnath* that he was reading.

Ananya sat down obediently.

"Why do you look so restless my dear, anything bothering you?"

Guruji's question startled Ananya.

Indeed she was preoccupied with the thought of her children left at the care of the stranger. But she never thought that her doubts showed on her face.

"No, nothing, *guruji*. I am just worried about Piyal. He has not been drinking enough water," Ananya lied.

"I see. Watch him through the day and if necessary, take him to the doctor in the evening," *guruji* said, concerned.

"What did you want to tell me *guruji*?" Ananya asked.

She wanted to return to her children quickly.

"Ananya, I want something from you today", *guruji* paused, took off his spectacles, and continued, "will you grant a request of mine?"

Ananya sat on the wooden stool, confused, her bewilderment showing.

Guruji smiled at her assuringly. "Don't worry child, its nothing big I am asking for," he said.

Ananya felt embarrassed.

"Order me *guruji*, you have every right to ask anything from me, I am so grateful to you for everything that you have done for me. It's my duty to fulfill every wish of yours," Ananya said thankfully.

"Don't talk about gratitude to me child. It's God who has helped you the way *He* wanted to, so you owe your gratitude to him. Moreover, you are a child of the ashram where we all do our duty to God and *His* children. We are here to serve humanity dear, nobody needs to feel grateful for anything," there was mild rebuke in his tone that made Ananya regret what she said.

"I am sorry guruji, I didn't mean it that way", she tried to apologize but *guruji* was already smiling at her.

"It's alright dear, now listen to what I have to say to you," he said.

Ananya looked at him attentively.

"Are you aware Ananya that somebody has come here along with your brother?" The question took her completely by surprise.

She had never expected *guruji* to bring up this question.

"Is he offended about my guests for some reason?" Ananya wondered.

"But we had already taken his permission before inviting JC and he had agreed most wholeheartedly," she recollected.

She nodded silently.

"Have you met that person yet?" *guruji* asked again.

"Not yet *guruji*. But why are you asking me this, is there any problem?" Ananya asked, apprehensively.

"That gentleman has come all the way here to meet you Ananya," he said.

"To meet me?"

Ananya sounded really astonished now.

"Nobody told me so, not even my brother!" her voice echoed her astonishment. "And why does he want to meet me *guruji*? Does he know me?" Now Ananya asked back.

"He didn't know you first but after coming to know you, he wants to meet you", *guruji* said with a mysterious smile.

"I am sorry, I don't think I understood what you said *guruj,i*" Ananya admitted innocently.

"I know you didn't understand but you will soon. For now, I just request you to meet him and listen patiently to whatever he has to say to you. You can take it as my advice also. Now you go dear, he must be waiting for you."

Ananya stood up . . . perplexed and confounded. She moved towards the door. She was just about to close the matted door behind her when, "Ananya", *guruji* called again.

She turned to face him.

"God bless you child," he said. There was deep affection in his voice that suddenly reminded her of her father and she felt a lump in her throat. Swallowing it down quickly, Ananya braced towards her hut.

It took her some moments to realize that she was actually running towards her hut, struggling to minimize the time that still stood between her and her destination.

Suddenly she knew who it was that was waiting for her, she knew why she was running, she knew where her destination lay.

When she reached the door of her hut, panting, he had his back towards her. He was rocking one of the infants in his arms and lisping away untiringly as though engrossed in pouring all the affection of his heart into his words.

"*Samarth*", Ananya pronounced the name with effort.

There was neither question nor astonishment in her voice, only an unfathomable stillness.

He turned around on hearing her voice. He looked just the same, Ananya noticed.

"Hey *Aan*, I could finally manage to make this little devil drink one full bottle of water . . . . but not before he offered stiff challenge you see.

Mom says I too was always a difficult child. Like father like son, right kiddo?" he said, rubbing his nose fondly with the child's.

Ananya watched dazed.

Samarth was moving towards her. She stood transfixed. The one year that stood between them seemed to have melted away magically.

Samarth seemed to pick up just from where she had left.

Ananya moved towards his outstretched arms. She was under a spell.

She couldn't resist his call and moved towards him.

Supporting his son in one arm, he pulled his *Aan* towards himself, with the other. Ananya relented. Almost instinctively her head rested on his chest. She took a deep breath and closed her eyes. She was home at last.

The trio stood there for a minute or so in complete silence except for some incomprehensible sounds of unreasonable delight from the infant in his father's arms.

Not a tear was shed. Not a question was asked. No explanation was offered. No rapturous outburst of ecstasy followed. The stillness of breath and the soft breeze of the late afternoon December witnessed the union of two souls.

A little distance away, through the door of the hut left ajar by Ananya, someone who had been watching the union with immense curiosity and expectation breathed a sigh of contentment and relief.

"Finally the family is complete", JC muttered smiling and crossed his chest in gratitude.

Chapter 25

Union and Separation
10ᵗʰ December, 1997

It was the first wedding in the Madhabpur ashram and the whole ashram had come alive. Though decided to be a quiet affair, it finally became quite pompous.

Samarth and Ananya had both wanted an unceremonious court—marriage but that would only delay the process by another month and *guruji* had insisted on the observance of the basic rituals, so they had to relent.

The children had decorated the temple beautifully with flowers and garlands and JC and the senior girls had taken care of the rest.

With Sister Kuhelika in charge of the overall supervision, Miss Mitra was kept busy by Piyal and Pihu.

The presence of Dr. Ghosh and Miss Mitra with their overflowing affection and blessings only intensified the stabbing pain that Ananya kept feeling within her . . . . She missed her parents, more than ever before.

"Don't worry *Aan*, everything will be fine . . . . just give them some time", Samarth had tried to comfort her, sensing her pain and Ananya desperately wanted to believe him.

Kuhu as always had a nice little surprise for her.

Hugging Siddharth and Vivek to her heart the trio swept each other in tears the moment Ananya was united with her children.

They had been invited by Sister Kuhelika to join the wedding celebrations.

"*Dadu* and *dida* are fine mom", they had assured Ananya "and they were very happy when we informed them about your marriage" Vivek said.

"Then why didn't they come with you both, were they waiting for an invitation?" Ananya asked hurt.

"Come on mom you can't expect them to be so exuberant in their expressions so soon, have patience and things will get to normal very soon." As Siddharth paused, Ananya couldn't help feeling a little amused, "who's the mom and who are the children I wonder" but she felt a comforting sense of security at the same time.

"My children are growing up fast", she thought contentedly.

The wedding fineries were sent as gifts by Katha and Sree who refused to yield to any protest from either Ananya or Samarth.

JC was treating the ashram and the local families outside the ashram to a special lunch that afternoon.

Guruji on his part had decided to conduct the sacred ceremony himself. In very short time this girl had won over his heart and he knew he would miss her very badly.

Clad in a red *banarasi* sari, with her forehead anointed in vermillion, accompanied by Samarth, dressed in a silk dhoti and embroidered kurta, all sent by the friends from abroad, when the newly wedded couple touched the feet of *Guruji*, Miss Mitra and Dr. Ghosh for blessings, there was not an eye that was dry.

The last one to embrace Ananya to her bosom was not Sister Kuhelika but *kuhu*, her childhood friend.

Years of practised restrain finally gave way to a cascade of emotions, gushing forth as tears of joy and pride for her friend whose days of patient struggle and faith had finally paid off. The throbbing of the two hearts became one as gratitude from one spilled over and blended with the joy flowing out of the other.

"Take care and stay well", were the only words whispered into her ear by her friend.

11th December, 1997

It's never easy to say goodbye and Ananya dreaded the moment.

But Samarth had to be back to work and the time had come to bid adieu.

Suddenly Ananya couldn't decide whether she was more happy to be united with her husband and children or more upset for having to leave behind her bigger and extended family here, in the remote village of Madhabpur.

As the old, white ambassador bumped along the uneven, half-roads of Madhabpur, towards the railway station, Ananya could only see obscurely through the back glass, a host of faces . . . innocent and matured, tear-laden and dry, sad and stoic, all overlapping one another and fast blurring into a misty vision.

Chapter 26

The defeated triumph

On their way home from the airport, all the three remained quiet. The journey from Madhabpur to Guwahati via Kolkata had been a tiring one. The silence was being broken from time to time only by queer sounds made by the twins, wriggling in their parents' laps as the taxi sped towards Samarth's Navinnagar residence.

The air around her was charged with tension and too much of apprehension. Suddenly Ananya found it very difficult to breathe in spite of the flourish of lush green all around her.

"A new challenge oh lord! How many more?" she sighed.

Samarth did not pretend to be relaxed. It was no use.

JC knew he did not have too much to do and yet he had to be there.

When the doorbell rang, quite expectedly Prabha came to open the door. Ishita had already left for school and the maid had not yet come in.

"Its Samarth", she knew, as she hurried towards the door.

Three days back he had left home in a hurry without explaining much and Prabha had taken it for granted that it was another of his usual office tours. But unlike the other times, this time her son hadn't called up to inform about his return. That had kept her a little worried through the last few days.

What awaited her at the other end of the door was not what she could have imagined in her wildest dream.

"*Ma*, this is Ananya . . . . my wife."

Prabha was sure she had not heard her son correct. She quizzically looked first at her son and then at the strange girl beside him, clad in red.

As her confounded gaze rested on the two infants, she heard JC's voice, "they are twins aunty."

He knew no further clarification was required.

Even with her eyes downcast, Ananya could feel the pain and shock of the elderly woman standing in front of her and she felt stung by guilt and remorse like never before.

"*Ma* . . . please *ma*, let me explain to you everything . . . ." Samarth intervened desperately.

For the first time Prabha showed some movement.

She turned and went inside without uttering a word, leaving the door ajar for them.

Samarth motioned Ananya to step inside.

JC placed their bags inside and turned to go. He knew the family needed to be left alone for sometime.

Before leaving he took Ananya's hand into his and gave her an assuring look.

"Time . . . sister . . . time", was all he said and hurried out.

The new bride stepped into her new household most unceremoniously. Without a single witness other than her husband, without the *mangalkalash* awaiting the *grihalakshmi* at the door—step, without any sound of joy or cheer, without the blowing of the sacred conch, Ananya made her *grihapravesh* in her husband's home.

Ishita turned out to be her only haven of refuge, especially in the absence of Samarth.

"Don't worry *boudi*, everything will be fine. *Ma* is just too shocked to react sensibly. *Dada* has never before hidden anything from her, that's why perhaps she can't take it." She had tried to comfort Ananya.

Ishita had liked her sister-in-law immediately. She had never quite approved of her brother's former choice though she had never articulated it.

That night when Samarth explained everything to Ishita, her heart swelled with pride for both of them.

"They exemplify the spirit of love, sacrifice and responsibility" she felt.

So long as Ishita was at home, the children would be in her care. But the moment she left for school, and Samarth for office, Ananya felt completely at sea.

Prabha had locked herself in her room with all her wounded feelings and faith, ever since her son had brought in his wife and their children.

"You people went so far ahead and never thought of telling me once! Why Samarth, why? I was not that bad a mother to you . . . . what did I do to deserve this?"

But the questions remained buried in the depths of her bleeding heart.

Her son had let her down very badly. He had shattered her faith.

She had not allowed any of them to enter her room though her heart ached and eyes flooded to hear her son.

"We need your forgiveness *ma*, we can never be happy without it . . . . at least for the sake of the children forgive us".

One night she had heard the girl implore, "Please come once *ma* and see your grandchildren . . . . I won't come in front of you if you don't want to see my face but don't deprive the innocents of your love, *ma*".

There was sincerity in her voice but the impact of the betrayal was still too strong to let her soften.

"Ishu said she had even been married once before!" she felt a fresh surge of disgust.

Winter gave way to spring and spring to a scorching summer.

But even the changing seasons could not melt the heart of a wounded mother.

Samarth had gradually stopped persuading his mother, leaving things helplessly to the care of time.

Even JC was taken aback. His assurances to Ananya were turning out to be an eluding dream.

He had restricted his visits and mostly met Samarth in his office or spoke to Ananya over the phone.

Thankfully Samarth's brother Ved had accepted Ananya very gladly and even from the far away Mumbai, where he was posted, he kept talking to his brother and sister-in-law, assuring them of his support all along.

But nothing mattered to Ananya other than Prabha's approval and she prayed hard everyday expecting to win it.

Piyal and Pihu were growing up fast. They had started crawling and slipped into their granny's room as often and as innocently as they did everywhere else in the house.

They were never sent out.

Soon their granny's room was where the children were found spending most of their time and Ananya knew that they had won back what their parents had lost.

"Life demands its final price from me now" thought Ananya one day.

It was a sultry May morning.

Samarth had left for office and Ishita for her school. Piyal and Pihu could be heard laughing and crying from their granny's room.

Ananya approached Prabha's room. Though the door was left open, she knew her entry there was prohibited. But today she had decided to intrude.

"*Ma*" Ananya called from the door-step. The elderly woman had her back to the door. She was too engrossed in playing with her grandchildren.

The unexpected voice made her swing back.

Ananya felt stung by her silent reproach at this intrusion.

As always she maintained her silence.

"I have come to take your leave *ma* and will not come back here anymore. But please don't punish your son because of me . . . . he cant bear this distance from you". Ananya paused, fighting to overcome her swelling emotions.

"I know my children will be best taken care of here", she paused and continued again "they are in their seventh month now and can manage without me if you are there."

There was a sigh from the other end of the room.

"We had both made a mistake but trust me this was the best way we thought we could make amends. Your son was not a coward *ma* . . . . he did not shy away from his responsibilities though he easily could have."

Ananya turned to leave. She felt she had spoken enough.

"Where will you go?"

Ananya's steps froze. Those were the first words her mother-in-law had spoken to her since she had stepped into that house.

Her voice quivered but she managed to say, "Madhabpur".

"Is that where your parents are?"

"No. That's the ashram where my children were born and where I got married."

"What about your parents?"

"They are in kolkata. Like you, they too couldn't forgive us."

The phone in the drawing room started ringing. Ananya didn't bother to answer it. She moved towards the main door with her small bag, aware of the gaze following her.

She felt very tempted to turn once and have a last look at her children but steeled herself immediately.

"Does Samarth know about your decision?"

Ananya had to stop and turn back to face her again.

"No. I'll inform him before he returns home."

The caller was persistent and the phone kept ringing.

But Ananya now made steadily for the door.

"Ananya".

She had to stop yet again. It was the first time that her mother-in-law had called her by her name.

"Yes *ma*?"

"Answer the phone and come to the kitchen to help me."

Then studying her stupefied expression, she added, "Hurry up, what are you waiting for? Today we are going to make prawn *malaikari* . . . . that's Samarth's favourite".

The Epilogue

The party

"Piyaaa l, it's almost six, the guests will start walking in any time . . . . hurry up and get ready", Ananya shouted impatiently.

"Coming mumma! Just give me a second; I swear I'll be there in a jiffy."

"What's taking you so long may I know and why have you kept the door shut? Pihu's clothes are lying in your room; even she can't change because of you."

"Oh mom she's always such a fuss and you are always taking her side", the complaint floated in from the other side of the door.

"Why can't she keep her things in her own room and leave me in peace? Now if you both leave me alone for just five more minutes, I promise to be out by then."

"All right but I hope your five minutes won't be by your dad's watch".

Piyal laughed behind the closed doors.

Ever since his childhood he had seen his mother struggling to teach values of punctuality to his father. He was always an obedient student only so long lessons were restricted to theory and did not demand practical application.

But anyway, time was indeed running out and he needed to hurry.

The wrapping was almost complete.

Piyal gave a last critical glance at his effort and looked quite satisfied.

He walked to the phone. There was a parallel connection in every room and he needed to be careful, lest mom should overhear.

He briskly dialed a number and waited impatiently for a couple of seconds.

"Hello, this is Piyal Bose, son of . . . . oh you remember me? Thank you so much Sir . . . . when can I expect you then?"

There was a moment's silence after which he was heard saying, "Thank you so much sir! I'll wait for you".

He replaced the phone, kept the wrapped packet in his own drawer under lock and key and quickly opened the door.

"Pihuuu, I'm through, you can come in and take your things," he shouted out to his sister before rushing away for a quick bath.

Downstairs the party was already flowing.

Prabha was beaming in spite of all the problems of arthritis and high blood sugar. Her children were all home and the house had come alive. She felt grateful to Ananya. It was all her doing.

Years back she had decided that this day, her wedding anniversary would be celebrated as a family reunion day and every member of the family had honored her decision. Demands of life and livelihood had taken them away from one another but they all made it a point to be home on this day.

Prabha was happy that years back she had not made the mistake of letting Ananya go. She had kept her family woven together.

"Sister, Siddharth and Vivek are already in town with their wives and kids, they just called me to inform that they'll be here in an hour or so," JC informed before hurrying away to supervise the caterer boys.

"Hey Aan, look who's here!" Samarth's voice made Ananya turn to see who it was.

Instantly her face lit up.

"Hullooo sweetheart", she cried and hugged a bright, blonde teenager to her bosom.

She was Kannan, Katha's daughter. Every year around this time she came to meet her grandparents in India and since the last two years she had been attending this party.

Kannan loved her mother's best friend. She had grown up hearing stories about their friendship and once every year she made it a point to visit her and renew the old ties of friendship.

Samarth's colleagues had started coming in and also the other friends.

Pihu had indeed taken after her mother. She played the perfect host.

Ananya felt proud of her daughter. It would have been very difficult to handle so many guests without her support.

Ishita deftly took care of the relatives. Not only did she enjoy this annual home-coming but was also ever willing to do every bit she could for her sister-in-law. She had been fond of her since day one and over the years she had loved her more than a sister.

Boudi had ever since been her biggest confidant and greatest support. Without her encouragement she would never have completed her PhD when everyone in the family insisted that she got married. She remembered how day after day *boudi* fought with *dada* when she kept turning down the marriage proposals one after the other.

She was past thirty and her mother and brothers were worried that they won't find a suitable match for an over-aged, over-qualified girl.

Only *boudi* thought otherwise.

Ishita remembered how her mother had often humiliated Ananya for casting a bad influence on her.

"Don't try to teach her things that you did", she often used to say rudely but *boudi* never took them to heart.

Runa chuckled to herself remembering how during her marriage, it was her mother who had been most boastfully telling her in-laws that her daughter had done her PhD and how hard she had worked for it.

"Attention! Ladies and gentlemen", the voice over the microphone coming from the direction of a small dais in the corner of the lawn, made everyone turn.

"Thanks to all of you for coming here tonight."

"What's Piyal doing with the microphone now?" Ananya wondered and tried reading Samarth's expression for a clue. There wasn't much hint there. He only looked amused. He always thought his children were very smart.

"You are all here to celebrate my parents' sixteenth wedding anniversary today and you have all finished your turns of congratulating them."

"What is this boy trying to do?" Ananya couldn't help feeling apprehensive. Pihu was very matured for her age and Piyal was just the opposite. His grandma had spoilt him completely. So Ananya simply couldn't trust Piyal with anything.

"But you know what? I am yet to give them a gift", he continued.

"Oh God is this what he is going to say calling the attention of the guests?" Ananya's irritation was rising.

"But tonight I have a surprise gift for my mom though I couldn't have managed it without dad's help. And I want to give it to her in front of all of you who love them."

Piyal's announcement sent a curious murmur among the guests.

"Oh so a conspiracy as usual against me", Ananya looked at her husband with mock anger and he smiled back.

"Hey mom, come here please", Piyal was calling her on the dais.

Ananya felt very embarrassed.

"Cummon auntie goooo . . . . he's calling you." It was Kannan.

When Ananya stood on the raised platform, her son handed her a small packet, carefully wrapped in a glossy gift wrapper.

There were demands from the crowd to open it and show the contents to everybody.

But her son wanted her to wait awhile before doing so. He invited an elderly gentleman to the dais and handed the microphone over to him.

"Good evening ladies and gentlemen, I am Prakash Sinha from *Westford publications*."

He introduced himself and continued. "Some time back I was shown a diary by a gentleman and his little son and asked to go through the contents. They wished to know if it was worth publishing."

He paused a while. Ananya couldn't understand what was going on. The gentleman continued, "A month back when I finished reading it I had decided that I was going to publish it. When I called up the father and the son to inform them about my decision, I was requested to hold the official announcement of bringing out the first copy till today and so have I come to hand over the first copy of the book to that little boy who has gifted it to his mother on her wedding anniversary, as you have just seen.

Now I would leave the stage for that fortunate mother and new writer to share her moment of surprise and joy with all her loved ones. I wish her more success as a writer in future", he climbed down handing over the microphone to Piyal as claps and cheers from the invitees filled the air around.

"Now unwrap it mom".

Ananya was too surprised to react. It was only when Samarth and Pihu joined her and Piyal on the dais that she started opening the gift wrapper, careful still not to tear her son's efforts.

A neatly bound book lay in her numb palm. The cover had a simple outline sketch of a woman

Through misty eyes she read the name on the cover-

Ananya-her journey of faith